Sparked by Love

PEGGY BIRD

author of *Falling Again* and *Believing Again*

CRIMSON
ROMANCE

F+W Media, Inc.

Published by
Crimson Romance
an imprint of F+W Media, Inc.
10151 Carver Road, Suite 200
Blue Ash, OH 45242. U.S.A.
www.crimsonromance.com

ISBN 10: 1-4405-7038-8
ISBN 13: 978-1-4405-7038-4
eISBN 10: 1-4405-7039-6
eISBN 13: 978-1-4405-7039-1

Cover art © iStockphoto.com/GMVozd

For the arts community in my hometown, Vancouver, Washington.

Acknowledgments

Most of the places and events in *Sparked by Love* are real. The city of Vancouver, Washington, where I live, does indeed have a huge Fourth of July event every year on the Historic Reserve. Officers' Row, where Shannon lives, is also real, as is the Land Bridge, built by the Confluence Project and adorned with Native American artist Lillian Pitt's cast glass masks and sculpture baskets.

However, I have taken liberties with a couple of things: most importantly, I blurred the lines of responsibility for the Fourth of July event by giving an imaginary character an imaginary job and tasks performed by many people over the course of the year before the event. To those people, I apologize and thank them for all their hard work to make this event the highlight of the summer for many of us.

Oh, and I regrew an oak tree on the parade grounds which was cut down some years ago because of disease so Leo would have a place to hang one of his fireworks.

Chapter One

Leo Wilson finished fire-polishing his latest glass vessel, maneuvered it out of the heat, and with the help of his studio mate, Giles Kaye, put it into an annealing oven. After the piece had been slowly brought down to room temperature, he'd inspect it and call the collector who'd commissioned the piece to come pick it up. If everything worked out, the sale would give him enough money to squeak through another month.

Leo didn't miss the scenes his ex-roommate/ex-girlfriend had thrown on a regular basis when she was working her way out of their relationship. In fact, he didn't miss much about their relationship at all. He did miss having someone to share expenses with, however. The financial pressure he'd been under for the past year or so was getting old. It was obvious he had to sell more art pieces, teach more classes, find a roommate, or take a part-time job. He wasn't sure which would present a bigger challenge—finding buyers for his work and students for his classes or finding a compatible roomie. A part-time job was possible, but that would give him less time to do his art, which meant fewer pieces to sell. But he was going to have to suck it up and pick one. Soon.

He was closing the door on the oven when Amanda St. Clair, the studio owner, called from her office. "Leo, when you have a chance, there's something here for you from the City of Vancouver."

She handed him a business-size envelope with City Hall, Vancouver, Washington as the return address when he got to her desk. "Another parking ticket?" she said. "Your visits to your buddies across the river are getting expensive."

"Luckily Vancouver's fines are a hell of a lot cheaper than Portland's. But I swear I paid the last one. And I haven't been at

Firehouse Glass for a couple months." He tapped the envelope on the palm of his hand. "Besides, how did they find me here? Before, the reminders came to my house. From DMV records they got from my license plate."

"You'll never find out what the letter says by osmosis. You have to read it," Amanda said, handing him the plastic gadget she used to slice open envelopes. "And this works better than staring at it and hoping it'll pop out all by itself."

He ripped through the top of the envelope and read the enclosed letter. "Oh. My. God." Leo could barely breathe. "Oh. My. God," he repeated. "I don't fucking believe this."

"What? What?" Amanda asked.

"Read this and tell me if I'm hallucinating." He shoved the letter across the desk at her.

She scanned it then looked up, a huge smile on her face. "Oh, my God, is right, Leo! You got the commission." She yelled, "Giles, come here. Quick."

Giles stuck his head into the office. "What's going on? Did one of you win the lottery or something?"

"Close," Amanda said, handing him the letter. "Look, Leo landed the grant from Vancouver."

"The $75,000 one?"

"The very one."

Although Leo hadn't taken his eyes off the letter Giles had returned to the desk, he didn't need to see her to hear the pride in Amanda's voice. His mother wouldn't sound any prouder at the news.

"Congratulations, Leo," Giles said. "This is great." He clapped his colleague on the back but Leo didn't respond. "Hey, did we lose you? Are you still on this planet?"

"Not sure," Leo croaked then cleared his throat. "I never thought this would happen." He picked up the letter, re-reading it, still not sure he believed the words. "This was such a long shot.

I figured my idea was too out there. But, look, they said … ah … where is it?" He ran his finger down the letter to the sentence he was looking for. "Here it is. 'Your design is bold, creative, and in the spirit of the region's arts as well as our annual celebration of Independence Day.'"

He didn't know which to be happy about first—having his art respected or having the financial picture he'd just been worrying about dramatically improved. For the moment, he decided to go with enjoying this chance to exhibit his art—he'd celebrate the money when he saw the first check.

"I'm going to have an art installation millions of people will see," he said.

"The number's more like tens of thousands," Giles said, "but for sure you'll get attention from the media. They always cover the fireworks at Fort Vancouver like a blanket. Biggest news story every Fourth of July."

"Don't rain on my parade, Giles. I've never landed anything like this before, and if I want to think there will be millions of people there, let me," Leo said.

"Well, there'll be a hell of a traffic jam on the I-5 Bridge if you're right. But you'll need more than congratulations to make this happen. If I recall the proposal, it's pretty complicated. What can I do to help you?"

"Yes, Leo, what do you need from the studio and from us?" Amanda asked.

"Give me a chance to absorb the news and we'll talk," he responded.

Leo made a quick phone call to the Clark County Arts Commission chair, whose name was on the letter, to officially accept the commission and make arrangements for all the paperwork he needed to fill out. Then he took his studio mates up on their offer to strategize. The three artists spent most of the morning planning how to get Leo's project accomplished. Specifically, how much could be done at the GlassCo studio and how much would have to be done in Vancouver, with his buddies at Firehouse Glass.

It was, as Giles had said, a complicated endeavor. Leo had proposed a large art installation on the grounds of the Historic Reserve where each year, the city of Vancouver, Washington, sponsored a huge party to celebrate the Fourth of July. There was music, art, and entertainment, food vendors and space to stroll around the grounds of an old army fort, now managed by the city. After dark, what was billed as the largest pyrotechnic display west of the Mississippi lit up the night sky. The fireworks could be heard, if not seen, all over the city as well as from the boats on the Columbia River and many parts of Portland, Oregon, which was right across the river from Vancouver.

The display had inspired Leo's proposal. Instead of a static, in-one-place exhibit of glass, he designed large and small glass fireworks to be installed in the trees and structures around the former parade grounds of the base where the crowds picnicked while they waited for the after-dark fireworks display.

Each burst would be made of slender tubes of glass in various sizes, shapes, and colors and would require careful installation to connect the pieces in the correct manner and secure them into place. Floodlit from below, Leo's fireworks would "go off" all evening as a computer controlling the lights would turn them off and on to simulate the moment when the shells burst into spectacular designs in the sky.

The project was large. It was complicated. It was expensive. And it was what Leo hoped would get his work the attention he'd been struggling for his whole career.

All he had to do was get a couple permits from the City of Vancouver, and he would be on his way. How hard could it be to get a couple of permits?

...

Three months later, Leo was at Firehouse Glass in Vancouver where he was creating some of the pieces for the display. The only official paper he had from the City of Vancouver were more parking tickets from his hours of working with his glass blower friends and forgetting to plug the meter.

Today they'd gotten the last of the pieces for one of the smaller fireworks completed and had spent the time they were working sympathizing with Leo about his difficulty getting the appropriate permissions.

"I mean, it's not like I'm misting the crowds with toxic waste, or endangering salmon or something. All I want to do is put up an art installation," he griped as he brought a gather of glass out of the glory hole. His attention was diverted to the job at hand for the next bit of time, but when the piece was shaped and in the kiln, he returned to his venting about the city.

"Have you guys had trouble with them about permits and things?" he asked.

Frank Steward, a longtime friend and colleague, shook his head. "No, but then we've never done anything more complex than be part of a team putting up a piece of public art in a city park. It's more complicated in the Reserve. Part of the property is managed by the city and there's National Park land involved in the visitor center and down near the recreated old fort. And there's a trust involved somehow, but I'm not sure how. It's kind of a special deal."

"Yeah, well, maybe if I'd known how difficult it would be to get the damn permits, I'd have thought twice about submitting my proposal," Leo said. "This woman who works for the city, this Shannon Morgan, is driving me nuts. She's supposed to be helping me get this done, but she puts up hurdles to keep me from accomplishing anything faster than I can jump over them. Everything I propose gets one of two responses: "no" or "not possible." They're the only words she knows. So far, she's turned down my request for some help from the city to install the glass, refused to get me a permit for the lighting, isn't sure if I can have access to the site early in the week before the Fourth to get the pieces up, and she's wavering about letting me use some of the sites I picked out but won't tell me why. She's a pain in the butt."

"Have you talked to her?"

"Of course I've talked to her. At least weekly for three months." Leo was indignant Frank would think he hadn't pursued this vigorously.

"I know you've *communicated* with her. I meant have you *talked* to her. You know, used your legendary skills with women to persuade her. Up close and in person." His buddy leered at him.

"Yeah, right. Legendary skills. You mean the ones getting rusty from lack of use since Cathy bailed on me?" Leo pursed his mouth and frowned. "But you might have hit on something. If I can't convince her with logic on the phone and in email, maybe I can dazzle her with bullshit in person. I've always had luck impressing the mothers of the women I date so maybe … "

"How do you know she's your mother's age?"

"I don't know for sure. But she fusses at what I want to do and tries to tell me what I can't do like my mom does. I mean, I already have one mother, and I love her. If I need a lecture, I can call her. I don't need a city employee filling in for her."

"Make an appointment with this Shannon Morgan. Show her what you're doing. Buy her lunch or something. Butter her up. Maybe you can soften her crustiness."

Leo thought about his friend's suggestion for a minute. "You're right. I need to see this woman in person to size her up. But no appointment. I want the element of surprise on my side. I'll go over to city hall right now. I have the design specs in the truck. I've got images on my phone of some of my other installations. I'll show her what I'm doing and see if it makes a difference."

Chapter Two

It was another crappy day for Shannon Morgan. She knew when she took the job as the community relations and public involvement coordinator for the city of Vancouver she'd have problems—and problem people—to deal with. That was practically the job description of community relations. But she hadn't expected her biggest problem would be Andy Larson, the boss from hell. The entire population of Vancouver gave her less trouble than he did. And all because he couldn't keep his dick in his pants.

He'd been fine at first, even helpful, if a bit creepy in his attention, standing too close when he talked to her, hanging over her shoulder when she was sitting at her desk. He'd asked her out for drinks a couple times to talk about work where they weren't distracted by what was going on around them. She'd politely said no every time and eventually the invitations stopped. Shannon had congratulated herself on putting an end to his unusual notice of her without hurting his feelings. However, when the annual bloodletting known as budget preparation began, Randy Andy proved her wrong. She wasn't home free.

Pressure from City Council to cut expenses was always part of the budget cycle, which meant almost everyone's job was on the chopping block each year. However, it was *not* part of the normal cycle to have your boss looking at your job the way a boa constrictor looks at a mouse. Shannon didn't figure it out at first because she was knee-deep in public meetings. But eventually, she was let in on the secret: the only way he could keep from cutting the job of the woman who had succumbed to his attentions as well as punish someone who hadn't, was to eliminate Shannon's job. Randy Andy was now after her, big time, but in a different way.

The temptation to rat Larson out to his wife was great. Better to be a rat who blabbed than a mouse who was lunch. Except it probably wouldn't save her job, although it would feel good. Maybe. In the end Shannon didn't make the call. Instead, she worked harder and harder, hoping to prove she was too valuable to lose.

Unfortunately, it didn't seem to be working. Larson had reamed her out at the staff meeting again today like he'd been doing every week for a month because she hadn't gotten her July Fourth assignments taken care of. It was wearing on her. Particularly since she'd been saddled with one of the least important—as far as she was concerned—parts of the Fourth of July event and the one making it very, very difficult to get things taken care of. She suspected her boss had assigned her to manage some flaky artist so she could fail. Then Randy Andy would ride to the rescue, proving he didn't need a community relations liaison, and have the justification he wanted to eliminate her position.

And the way things were going it wasn't too hard to see how she could fail. Her boss had told her little about the art project she'd been assigned to facilitate other than this guy wanted to hang glass around the parade grounds in the Historic Reserve. No matter how many times she asked for it, she'd never seen the proposal the artist—Leo Wilson was his name—had made to the Community Foundation, although rumor had it, he'd gotten a boatload of money from them to finance it. She doubted that people who were at the event for the music and the fireworks would pay much attention to some arty-farty display, no matter what it looked like. But she had to make it work regardless of her opinion.

It wasn't easy. Apparently the artist thought having the grant meant she was to say "yes" to any demand he made because he was such an important *artiste*, and everyone should kowtow to him. He didn't understand she had already simplified the process at the request of the County Arts Commission to the point where, if she did much more trimming of requirements, she'd piss off a whole lot of people from this Washington to the one in the District of Columbia because she'd skirted one too many of the convoluted local, state, and federal regulations governing the Reserve.

It made her brain explode to think about it. First, this guy told her he wanted to hang glass—glass, mind you—from places like the bandstand where dozens of groups would be performing off and on all day. Not that he seemed to care if he put people at risk with the stupid glass. And her in danger of being reprimanded for allowing it.

Then he wanted to use city employees to help him. The maintenance crews always clocked massive overtime getting ready for the Fourth. Adding additional hours would strain the budget even more. Did he not have any idea how much work it took to get the huge event ready for the crowds?

Oh, and he wanted to hang some of his stuff around the Fort Vancouver Visitors Center, which meant having to deal with the Park Service. Things were quiet between the city and the Park Service right now. The last thing she wanted was to reignite the turf wars between the city, the Park Service and the Trust.

Leo Wilson was simply maddening. Why a supposedly intelligent adult didn't understand the need for a few simple rules to protect one of the most important historic treasures in the region, she didn't understand. Although it was possible he didn't appreciate the value of the site—Portlanders didn't pay much attention to what went on in Vancouver.

More likely, it was because of his sex. She'd had more than her share of difficulties with his flavor of the human species. The latest problem being her boss, of course. The longest running one was her father, who'd left her mother when Shannon was a kid, only to drift in and out of her life at inopportune moments ever since, running hot and cold over whether he wanted to be a father. No matter how hard Shannon tried—and she'd done just about everything she could think of—her father never seemed to stick around for very long. It had been several years since she'd last seen him, leaving a hole in her life she wanted to be filled.

Then there was Jeremy Vincent, her ex-boyfriend. Out of the blue a year or so ago, he decided he needed "space" and went off hiking the Himalayas. Well, actually the Pacific Crest Trail but same-same. She hadn't heard from him since. He'd drifted away, too, just like her father had. Sometimes she thought she didn't care that Jeremy had left. On rare occasions, she almost convinced herself she wanted him back, although the thought didn't usually last long. Most of the time, she was just pissed off because he left without telling her the real reason.

Leo Wilson was obviously a pain in the butt like so many of the other men she'd known. She was beginning to wonder if she'd ever find the kind she heard other women sigh over. So far, she'd come up empty.

Whatever the reason, Leo Wilson was being so demanding she had to get the damn art installation squared away before she caught any more flack from her boss. It was only three and a half months until July and time was short. As soon as she'd escaped the staff meeting, she called Wilson's studio in Portland to see if he'd gotten her last message and was told he was out of the studio for the day.

Typical. His artistic muse probably slept in so he got to play hooky.

Four hours, a dozen phone calls, and one conference call about an upcoming set of public meetings later, Shannon was about to have a power bar lunch while she cleared her desk of all the paper that had accumulated since she'd arrived. A man clearing his throat behind her interrupted her sorting and recycling.

"Uh … excuse me. Sorry to interrupt. Can you help me?" The deep male voice was smooth and soft.

Without looking to see who was asking, she said, "What can I do for you?"

Then she turned and looked up. Thank God she'd replied before she did because if she'd seen him before she tried to speak, she'd have been unable.

Standing in the entrance to her cubical was a really good-looking man. He was tall, at least six feet, maybe taller. His dark hair, cut short-ish on the back and sides, fell across his forehead calling attention to intensely blue eyes. The beginning of crinkles around those eyes, and slight lines around his mouth, showed he smiled a lot, although not so much at the moment. His prominent jawline was dusted with a day's worth of dark stubble, a look she didn't usually like, but for him she might be willing to make an exception. He was that cute.

When she could tear herself away from his face, she looked over the rest of him—shoulders she was sure would look even more amazing if he took off the black T-shirt he was wearing. A tattoo of interwoven lines around his impressive right bicep peeked out from under the T-shirt sleeve. And his hands. They were large and nicely shaped, the thumbs hooked into the pockets of black jeans caressing a trim waist, slim hips, and long legs ending in heavy work boots.

Then his smile broadened and a merely good-looking man turned into Adonis in jeans. The guy was seriously hot. If she had been in the market for a new man in her life, he might fill the bill. Okay, with the way he filled those jeans, he would definitely be a candidate. It was possible he could be the one to revive her faith in men. If she was looking for someone to do that. Maybe she should think about it. With a guy this hot, it could be worth a try. If only he was looking for her so she could start a conversation and see if he was as interesting to talk to as he was to look at.

●●●

Why wasn't she the woman he'd been dealing with? She looked as cool and delectable as a dish of ice cream, not at all like the mean, bossy, bitter bureaucrat he was looking for. This woman was young, probably in her mid to late twenties, his age. And she was beautiful. Long hair the color of honey was held back from her face with some sort of clip, with enough tendrils escaping to frame her face with tiny bits of curls. Brown eyes with an intelligent look in them were surrounded by thick lashes, which would probably brush her cheekbones when she closed them. A lush mouth with just the right amount of pink lip stuff on it to attract his attention and make him want to kiss it off. When she'd swiveled in her chair to face him, he saw enough of her body to know the skirt and top she was wearing did little to disguise a curvaceous body and a pair of great legs.

"I'm looking for Shannon Morgan. I thought the receptionist said she was down here someplace." He looked around one more time. "But maybe I went the wrong way." He turned to leave.

"Wait. You're looking for Shannon Morgan? That's me. What can I do for you?" she repeated.

Holy hell. She *was* the woman he'd been dealing with. "I'm Leo Wilson, the glass blower. We've been communicating about my art installation for the Fourth of July. I thought maybe it would make things work better if we met in person." He held out his hand to her.

She seemed to hesitate for a moment, then stood up. If he pulled her close, he figured she'd almost reach his shoulder. And he definitely wanted to pull her close. He could see now the body he'd glimpsed had all the right curves in all the right places. Places he was sure would fit nicely against him.

She put out her hand. It was small and soft, making him only too aware of the calluses on his and the probability it wasn't as clean at the moment as hers was. He didn't let go of her hand immediately, enjoying the contact.

"Leo Wilson? You're not what I expected," she said. "Not what I expected at all." Her face reddened. "I'm sorry. I mean, I thought maybe you were a lot older. You know, a mid-career … I don't know … something." She pulled her hand away from his.

He didn't want to let go but reluctantly did. "Yeah, you're not exactly the bureaucrat I expected either." He smiled. "So, we agree neither fits the other's stereotype. Maybe we should start this whole thing over again."

"Okay," she said, "I'll reintroduce myself. I'm … "

"No, I get the part where you're Shannon Morgan and I'm Leo Wilson. I meant talking about my project."

She laughed. "Good idea. Where shall we start?"

He thought for a moment. "Can you leave your desk for a half hour or so?"

"I guess. To do what?"

"Walk with me to the fort and around the parade grounds and let me show you what I have in mind."

Chapter Three

Spending her lunch break with a gorgeous guy on a reasonably decent spring day wasn't the worst duty Shannon had ever pulled. Besides, the walk from city hall to the Historic Reserve offered her the opportunity to tell him about this special place. She wanted him to understand how important it was to the city and to the region and why she cared so much. So as they made their way to the fort, along city streets and a freeway overpass, she gave him the whole history of the district, assuming he didn't know the story.

She started with the original owners, the Hudson's Bay Company, who built the fort to keep the English company's trade goods *in* rather than to keep hostiles *out*. The National Park Service had reconstructed the fort and did excavations around the site to learn more about that part of the Reserve's history.

After the Americans took over what became the Washington Territory, the army used the site for a century until they consolidated posts, closing this one. That was when the city came into the picture. First the homes on Officers' Row, some of them built as far back as 1846, were purchased and rehabbed into a restaurant, a meeting facility, office space, and rental homes. Then the city and a group of citizens took over the mostly WWII homes and buildings on the rest of the defunct army post with the idea of also making them community assets.

Leo, it turned out, wasn't as unaware as she assumed. In fact, he surprised her with what he added to her travelogue. He knew Ulysses S. Grant, George C. Marshall, and O.O. Howard had been assigned there and had buildings named for them. He asked where the Russian aviators landed who were the first to fly across the North Pacific. And he enthusiastically talked about the hopes the arts community in Vancouver had for a performing arts center or an arts incubator space in some of the WWII buildings. He even knew about the problems that flared up occasionally between the three entities that managed the land.

The more they talked, the more her opinion of him crept upward. The tipping point was when, as they passed the small gazebo marking one entrance to the Historic Reserve, he said, "As long as we're here, I might as well bring up something I haven't asked you about so far. I need some advice. I'd originally planned a small installation inside each of the three entrance gazebos as a way to introduce the project to people. Whet their curiosity. But the more I walk around the grounds, the more I wonder. First, will people really notice them? I mean, you have those beautiful hanging baskets of flowers there and I'm not sure the glass adds anything. Second, are they too far away from the main venue and likely to be targets for vandals? What do you think?"

"The flower baskets might obstruct the installation but we could move them for the Fourth. I like the idea of having a piece there. Maybe with a sign about what they can look for on the parade ground?"

"Yeah, I plan on several signs as well as some handout materials."

"Safety is the most important concern for me, both for your glass and the people coming and going. On the Fourth itself, I don't think there'll be a problem. The streets are blocked to vehicular traffic and there'll be someone at the gazebos throughout the event. Everyone has to stop there to pay the entrance fee so they'd see your work. The only possible problem is the gazebo to the south. There's a gate there, too, but it's more isolated before the road is blocked off than the two on Evergreen are."

She frowned. "Installing them in advance could create a target for vandals. Although most people drive past here rather than walk, which might help."

"Entrance gates. Good to know. Maybe if I put these pieces up last, like the day before or the morning of ... and maybe just on the two along here." He indicated the road they were walking along. "I'll have to think about it. Thanks." He looked down at her and smiled. For the second time, it was a really big, genuine smile. He had these cute dimples, and with the way his eyes crinkled when he smiled, it about buckled her knees.

She gulped and tried to get her mouth, which was suddenly quite dry, to work. "You know, I've never seen the proposal you made to the Community Foundation. Do you happen to have an extra copy I could look at?"

"Are you shit … kidding me? You didn't get the copy I submitted to the city when I applied for the permits?"

"No, I didn't."

"No wonder you haven't known what I've been talking about. I was sure you already knew, so I never went into too much detail. I apologize. You should complain to your boss."

Yeah, right. Like complaining would help. He probably kept it from me deliberately. "If you submitted one, I should be able to track it down."

"You won't have to. I have a copy in my truck along with the drawings I use to make the pieces I'll need. When we go back, I'll get it for you."

By this time, they'd reached the split rail fence surrounding the old parade grounds. Even in the cool spring weather there were dog walkers and parents with small children scattered around the grounds enjoying the urban green space.

Leo leaned against a post and rested one foot on the bottom rail of the fence. He dug out his smartphone and touched the screen. As he flipped through a file, he gestured to her. "Come take a look at these images. This'll give you a visual of what I'm proposing."

Shannon tried to see the screen without standing too close to him, but it wasn't possible. To see what he wanted her to see, she had to be almost snuggled up to him, close enough to be warmed by the heat of his body. She could almost feel the rumble of his voice when he spoke. Could smell his aftershave or body wash or whatever it was that smelled spicy and male. Was close enough to see the details of his tattoo. Was close enough to be unnerved.

She gave herself a mental shake. This was work, not a meet-up from Match.com. She better get her game face on and concentrate on the small screen in his hand, not on how he smelled or looked or sounded.

Once she saw what he wanted her to look at, however, how he smelled and sounded became secondary to what she was seeing on his phone. She was riveted. What he was showing her was stunning.

He flicked through image after image of what he said was a recent installation. From long, slender, curved cylinders of glass in shades of yellow and white, Leo had created the impression of a large, chrysanthemum-like flower. The petals started on the outside as large and loosely spaced. Gradually, the layers got smaller and tighter until the center was a completely enclosed round of glass rods. The flower sat on a nest of green glass leaves and appeared to float on the water in a formal garden.

"My idea for the fireworks is to shape them somewhat like the flower except turn it upside down."

"It's beautiful. I've never seen anything like it." She looked up at him, probably looking like a grinning fool.

He grinned back. "Thanks. For the installation here, each piece will hang from a structure or a tree and be lit from below and maybe from above. I'm going to have to experiment to see how it looks. The lights will be controlled by a computer and will be turned off and on in a random sequence so it looks like the glass fireworks are being set off."

"The question I've had is how you're going to rig the lights. Won't there be cords all over the place?"

"No, I want it to be like the real fireworks. Like it mysteriously happens. I'll program my laptop to signal the spots wirelessly. No electrical cords for people to trip over or spoil the effect."

"Oh, my God, now I get it. It'll look like magic."

"That's the plan." He turned the phone off and put his hand at the small of her back. "Let me show you where I think the best places will be for the installations."

Focused on the warmth and pressure of his hand on her back, Shannon stumbled when her heel caught in a patch of uneven ground. He grabbed her by the waist to keep her from falling, pulling her close to him. It may have saved her from a hard landing, but it also made the distraction factor multiply by about ten. His arm felt good around her. His body was solid and muscled. He could make you feel secure, safe, protected with merely his arm around you.

What was she thinking? She reminded herself once again she was working here, a fact getting harder and harder to keep in mind.

Moving out of his reach, she said, "Where do you want to go first?"

...

Where did he want to go? Anyplace where he'd have a chance to touch her again. Then anywhere he could move on to something more like kissing her.

Leo looked around the parade grounds hoping the way to the bandstand was over rough ground, giving him another excuse for holding her. He wanted to feel the way she trembled again when he put his arm around her. Wanted to smell her flowery shampoo and see once more the look on her face when she first beheld his work. Wanted to find out for sure if he was right—she wasn't shivering from the cool spring air. She was as affected by the chemistry between them as he was.

Frank had been right, although for the wrong reason. This meeting should have taken place weeks ago. Not to get his art installation straightened out but to meet Shannon Morgan as up close and as personal as he could make it. He couldn't remember the last time a woman had turned his crank like she did. And he'd wasted time communicating with her on the phone and through email!

He must have looked like the idiot he felt like because she was staring at him with a puzzled look on her face. Back to business, then.

"How 'bout we start with the one you have the biggest problem with … the bandstand?" On an impulse, he held out his hand. "Here, hold on. Your heels might catch again in the grass. Don't want you to fall." He was surprised when she readily took it and held on tight.

Sadly—for him—the ground was level from the fence to the bandstand, so he didn't have a chance to hold her close again. And as soon as they got to their destination, she dropped his hand and bounded up the steps. He followed.

"So, you're concerned about the safety of the glass … " he began.

"The safety of your work and the safety of the groups who'll be performing here," she finished. "We have small musical groups, the occasional puppet show, singers, jugglers … "

"Fire eaters? Lions and tigers and bears, oh, my?"

She couldn't suppress her laugh. "Close. How far down will the glass hang?"

"My plan was to suspend the piece so it hung low enough to be seen from outside the structure and fence it off so people wouldn't be able to get into the gazebo. It would be the centerpiece of the exhibit, with signs around it explaining what it was all about, maybe have a display table next to it where I could talk to people about the installation. But the idea is obviously not gonna work."

"No, but I see what you're trying to achieve. Where else could you make it work?" She swept her eyes around the grounds. "What about those two big oak trees? Would one of them do? They're close enough to the bandstand to be central to all the activities and the pieces would be high enough to be out of reach of anyone who wanted to bat them around."

He jogged over to the two trees, which were spaced about twenty yards apart and circled them, looking up into the branches of what must have been hundred-year-old trees. "How about this—how about I suspend wire cable from one tree to another and hang the firework in between them? I'd set up an information booth under it and staff it all day."

"Do you think it'll work?"

"Not sure but if it's okay with you and whoever else has to approve, I'd like to give it a try. If I don't think it'll be secure, I'll suspend two smaller ones from the two trees to flank the information booth."

"Done. Now, what else do you have planned?" With the biggest problem out of the way, she seemed to visibly relax.

For the next half hour, they traipsed around the grounds as Leo showed her the places he'd selected as possible sites for his installation. From the area around the National Park visitor center on the northeast corner to the area on the south edge of the ground where the picnic tables were located, to the trees along Evergreen Boulevard, he showed her all the possibilities. Shannon made notes and took photos with her phone, but the more they tramped around and talked, the more she seemed open to any and all of his ideas.

Eventually she said, "I better get back to my desk. I really appreciate your doing this. I should have thought to ask you to show me around long ago. It would have made things much easier. With a better idea about what and where you plan to work, I know exactly who needs to sign off on it. I should be able to get it done in ten days, maybe less."

"Thanks. And I'm the one who should have offered a tour when I first contacted you. I'm sorry I didn't. For a lot of reasons."

She glanced down at the ground then back up, her eyes half hidden by her long lashes. "A lot of reasons?"

"Yeah. And not all of them professional." Leo let the sentence hang in the air like one of his fireworks for three or four breaths before saying, "Look, this may be inappropriate but the next time I'm in Vancouver working at Firehouse Glass, can I take you out to lunch?"

"I'd like to," she began, "but I'm not sure … " She let the sentence fade off. She was obviously going to say no but the expression on her face looked like she was reluctant to do so.

"It's okay. I get it. You're in charge of getting my work approved, and I don't want it to look like I'm trying to influence you inappropriately." He cocked his head and half-smiled. "Maybe after everything's all settled … ?"

She smiled back. "Sounds good."

Chapter Four

A week later, Shannon had the excuse she needed to make the phone call she'd been looking forward to. But now that she had a reason to contact Leo, no one seemed to be on the other end of the line. Finally, after about a dozen rings, a woman answered and said abruptly, "GlassCo."

"Is Leo Wilson there?"

"Yes, but he's in the middle of something right now. Can he call you back?"

"Sure. Tell him Shannon Morgan from the city of Vancouver …"

"Wait, I think he's finished. Hold on."

Before Shannon could protest the interruption of his work, she heard the woman yell, "Leo, Shannon Morgan's on the line. From Vancouver. Shall I take a message or can you come to the phone?"

Leo's reply was somewhat muffled but she thought he said, "I know who Shannon is, Amanda. I'll talk to her now."

In a few seconds, he said, "Hey, Shannon. Sorry to keep you waiting. I was finishing up a piece for one of the fireworks."

"I shouldn't be interrupting you at work. I could have emailed, but I was so excited about getting it all done I decided to call instead. Thought you'd want to know right away. As soon as you could, I mean." She realized she was babbling, took a deep breath, and started over. "What I meant to say is, all the permits and permissions came through, and I wondered if you'd like to take a look at them and make sure I got it all right."

"When?"

"When? You mean, when to see them?" God, she sounded like an idiot. She never had this problem talking to anyone else she dealt with.

"Yes, that's what I mean." His voice was low and soft; it felt sweet, like warm chocolate syrup pouring over her. It also sounded sexy and slightly amused.

"Today? Tomorrow? What's good for you?" she asked.

"Are you free for lunch today?"

He sounded as anxious as she was to get together again. "Yes, I am. How about eleven forty-five at the entrance to city hall?"

"See you then." He paused for a second before saying, "And, Shannon? Thanks for making this happen."

"Just doing my job, but you're welcome."

• • •

Leo was ten minutes early and spent the time looking around the lobby of Vancouver's city hall. Built in 2008 as the new headquarters for the city's daily newspaper, a bad economy and the long, slow slide of the newspaper business had led the local owners of *The Columbian* to file for bankruptcy, return to their old offices, and let the bank sell the new one.

It made a stunning civic building. If the glass front wall and etched glass panels inside hadn't commanded Leo's attention, the three-story atrium lobby would have. He got so lost in inspecting the building, he forgot to watch the people walking by.

Then he heard, "Nice building, isn't it?" And there she was, in a slim chocolate brown wrap skirt with big buckles down one side and a white blouse with narrow tan stripes. With her hair in loose waves over her shoulders and heels giving her an extra few inches in height, she looked all business and hot as hell at the same time. All he could think was how much he wanted to unbuckle those fasteners and see what was under the skirt.

He was glad he'd gone back to his house before he headed for Vancouver and changed into neatly pressed jeans and a collarless shirt.

"Maybe not as historic as Portland's city hall but a lot more impressive when you enter. And it's a more functional workspace, too, I imagine," he answered.

"It's wonderful, much classier than the old city hall. I think this architecture will wear better than the seventies style of our former offices. I feel sorry for the newspaper staff, though. They were only in here long enough to get to like it before they had to move out." She started toward the door.

Asking, "Where am I taking you for lunch?" he followed.

"How do you feel about food trucks?"

"Love them but I was thinking something more … "

"Vancouver only has one so far—Mighty Bowl. They move from place to place and today they're right across the street near Esther Short Park. It's a gorgeous day; we can eat in the park and enjoy the sun."

He reached ahead of her and pushed opened the door. "Show me the way."

Ten minutes later they were eating their veggies and rice lunch, sitting along the edge of a fountain full of kids wading in the still chilly water. "So, does this measure up to the cart culture in Portland?" Shannon asked.

"Absolutely. It's delicious." He nodded toward the file folder she had tucked under her. "Are the permits and permissions in there?"

"Yup. You can take a look when you're finished eating. One thing didn't work out. Your idea to string wire cable for a large firework between the two oaks? The urban forestry staff vetoed it. They're okay with you hanging a small one in each tree—they have a specified weight limit in the permit—but they turned down one big one on a cable. Too much weight, they say, for such old trees."

"I'm not surprised. It was a spur of the moment idea. I didn't put any research into it. So, we go with two small ones, then, and a canopy over an information desk between the two. Maybe put some literature out from your tree guys so folks know it's okay to do what I've done."

"So you're not upset?" Shannon had a little crease between her eyes—a frown, really. He'd noticed it before when he thought she was worried about what his response would be.

"If that's the only problem, I'm a happy camper." The crease didn't disappear, so he looked around for something else to talk about to put her at ease. "I've never been in this park before. Which is odd since Firehouse is only a couple blocks away. It's beautiful. And it has a killer bandstand."

She seemed to relax a little as she talked. "We have summer concerts there. Pink Martini's been here, Patrick Lamb, Aaron Meyer, Curtis Salgado, sometimes the Vancouver Symphony."

"Do you go to the concerts?" Leo watched closely to see if the frown reappeared.

"As many as I can. Assuming the weather's good. I'm not much for sitting in the rain or in one hundred degree heat."

"I'm not either. Would you be up for some company at one of the concerts if the weather's nice?" He ducked his head apologetically. "I should probably have asked first if you already have someone to go with."

She shrugged her shoulders. "Used to. Don't anymore." She looked up from under those incredible eyelashes and smiled. "I'd love company. Do you want me to send you the schedule when it comes out?"

Wanting to see her outside work, Leo pushed his advantage. "Or do I have to wait until summer to do something with you other than discuss work?"

This time she laughed. "No, not if you don't want to."

"Good. Because summer's a long way off. This weekend is closer. Could we start then? Maybe a movie. Do you like movies as well as concerts?"

"Absolutely. There's a new indie movie at the Living Room Theater off Burnside—something about living in a war zone. It sounds interesting."

"You're on. What time should I pick you up?"

"I'll meet you there if you—"

"My mama raised me right. Where do you live and how do I get there? I know a bit about downtown Vancouver but not much else about the place."

"No problem. You've already been close to where I live—I rent one of the townhouses on Officers' Row, across from the parade grounds."

The arrangements for the movie settled, their lunches finished, and all the paperwork signed, Leo walked Shannon across the street to city hall. "Thanks for taking care of all this," he said, indicating the folder of permits she was carrying.

"Like I said, it's part of my job. I'll have copies made and mail them to you."

"And I'll see you Saturday."

• • •

The movie was a disappointment but the evening wasn't. After they left the theater they wandered across Burnside Street to Portland's iconic bookstore and got lost in the stacks for an hour or so before having dinner at a nearby Thai restaurant. Shannon couldn't remember the last time she'd laughed so much or felt so comfortable being with someone, the last time an evening out had been so good. Honestly? The last time she'd had an evening out at all, let alone one this much fun.

They held hands like high-school sweethearts as they walked along the sidewalks, and he didn't do more than gently kiss her when he took her home. It was a kiss as sweet as the handholding had been. Affectionate but not demanding, holding her close enough so she could enjoy the feel of male muscle but not so aggressive he turned her off. Somehow, Leo knew instinctively exactly how to impress her.

There was chemistry between them, she had to admit. Chemistry and common interests and a lot of laughing. If she wasn't careful, she could begin to want to see more of him, even though he hadn't said anything about repeating the evening. Although maybe having the temptation to get involved with yet another man who could break her heart was best left out of arm's reach. She wasn't sure she could handle that kind of hurt again.

• • •

She was so sweet. Sweet and sexy and smart and fun to be with. She wasn't fussy and demanding, wasn't afraid to show she was enjoying herself; she made him laugh. If there was an opposite of his ex, Shannon was it. Their first evening together had been everything Leo had wanted it to be and more.

It took all the control he had to keep from kissing her silly when he took her home, but he knew better. He didn't think she was the kind of woman who got in too deep too soon. She was smarter. And, given the last time he'd jumped in too fast and ended up with the fuzzy end of the lollipop, he would be better off being smart about it himself. If his experience with Cathy had taught him nothing else, it had taught him to wade into these waters slowly, enjoying the build-up and making sure he wasn't in over his head.

But if the way his dick reacted to one gentle kiss tonight was any indication, it wasn't going to be easy.

Chapter Five

Shannon got an email from Leo on Monday with an attached review of the movie they'd seen the weekend before. His message said they should have found it before they wasted two hours watching a bad movie. On Tuesday, she got a second email saying he'd be in Vancouver later in the week and would drop by. She didn't know if he meant at work or at home. However, she was so busy getting ready for the public meetings she was in charge of on Wednesday and Thursday, she didn't have time to think about it.

The meeting on Thursday began at four. It was contentious, exhausting, and seemed like it would never end. It was close to eight o'clock when she dragged her tired body over the freeway bridge and onto Officers' Row, happy to be in sight of home. She was almost there when she saw lights on the parade ground across the street. Stopping to watch in the darkening night, she saw what appeared to be a big spotlight pointed up into one of the oaks, circling it, before moving to another tree. She couldn't work out what was going on until she recognized the trees as the same ones Leo was considering for his fireworks installation.

Then she remembered the message she'd gotten on Tuesday. He said the next step was experimenting with lighting. That's what was going on. Her energy suddenly renewed, she walked through a gap in the split rail fence and strode toward the moving light. When she was within shouting distance she yelled, "Hey! You with the light! Do you have a permit?" She had a hard time keeping the laugh out of her voice.

It got a lot easier to be serious when the beam from the spot stopped her cold, forcing her to shield her eyes with her arm to keep from being temporarily blinded.

"Shannon! Oh, my God, I'm sorry." Leo turned off the light. He apologized all the way across the parade ground as he ran toward her. "I didn't mean to … I mean, I didn't know … I'm so sorry. Are you okay?" When he got to her, he hugged her close and ran his fingers over her face, as if trying to see whether the light had actually burned her.

"I'm fine." She blinked a few times to get him into focus. "What are you up to other than blinding a local resident with your spot?"

"Again—apology. I didn't think. I wanted to see who was yelling at me about permits." He grinned. "I should have known it was you."

"I'm not sure a permit is required for lighting trees but I'll check tomorrow. Let's get back to what you're up to."

"I'm looking for the best places to hang the glass. Trying to see how the light shadows or accents specific places in the trees. I called you at work late this afternoon to see if you'd have dinner with me before I started my experimenting but got your out-of-office message. Then there was no answer when I knocked at your door an hour ago."

"I've had two evenings of hellish public meetings with people yelling about the parking fines and where you can park. Hardly been at my desk all week trying to get this organized"

"Please don't tell me you're going to raise the fines. This is the only place in the whole region I can afford the parking tickets."

"Sorry. Afraid they're proposing to raise both the fines and the meter costs."

"Damn. I'll have to pay more attention, won't I?" He peered down at her. "You sound tired."

"I am. It's been some week."

"I was going to ask you to go get a beer with me when I'm finished, but I'm guessing the answer would be 'not tonight.'"

"You're right. I don't feel much like a noisy bar, but why don't you come over to my place when you're done and have a beer there?"

"Ten minutes, maybe, and I'll have what I need. Okay?"

"See you in ten."

• • •

Returning to his spotlight experiments, Leo found it difficult to remember what the hell he needed to do that was more important than being with Shannon. He looked around at the trees. Looked over at her house. Looked back at the trees. No contest. He'd rather be with her. The trees could wait.

When he approached her house, there were no lights on, either outside or in. He wondered if she'd changed her mind and gone to bed. Bed. Now there was a thought he shouldn't get imbedded … shit … even the word describing what he shouldn't be thinking about contained it. Bed. Shannon in one. His. Hers. He wasn't picky. The more he told himself to stop, the more he became obsessed with the vision of Shannon in his arms … naked.

Telling himself to slow down hadn't worked, in spite of his determination to be careful about how fast he got involved with her. The part of his brain trying to put on the brakes was being overridden by the other part—the one thinking of things like what she wore to bed. Would it be a cute little nightgown, all ruffles and lace, or pajamas? Or would he luck out and discover she slept nude? He could see her, naked, her hair spread out on the pillow, her hands reaching for him …

Jesus. There it was again. He hadn't given her more than a chaste good night peck on the cheek, and he already had them in bed. If this was slow, he wondered what the hell fast was.

As he walked up the path to her house, he saw her waiting in the shadows on a porch swing. At least he could stop picturing her in bed for a few minutes.

She smiled at him as he approached, and he took the steps two at a time to get to her as fast as he could.

"Got what you needed?" she asked.

"I think so." He sat next to her. "I may have to come back, but I'm pretty sure I have a better idea of what will go where."

"You know, when I was first given this assignment, all I could think was, oh, right. Hang some glass in the trees. Big deal. But since we've talked about it, since you've explained what you're trying to achieve and I've read your proposal, I realize it *is* a big deal. I apologize for not taking it seriously at first. It's a lot more complex, more complicated than I ever realized."

"No apology needed. How could you make sense of it when you didn't have the proposal to look at? Did you ever figure out why you didn't get a copy of it?"

She sighed. "I didn't have to figure it out. I'm pretty sure I know. My boss has to make budget cuts so he's trying to eliminate my position to save someone else's job. There's this woman he's involved with ... Anyway, I think he figures if I screw up the biggest event on the civic calendar and he has to save it, he'll have a reason to do what he wants. You were merely the means to an end."

"Fucker. Sorry ... "

"Don't apologize. You're right. He is a sorry-ass fucker. But he's the sorry-ass fucker I have to deal with it. However, with your project settled, all I have to do is get the contracts signed with a couple dozen vendors, and the prelims for the Fourth are finished. Then I can get back to fending off people who don't want to pay higher meter rates."

He laughed. "Tell me when those meetings are and I'll be there with a pitchfork and torch myself."

"Too late. The comment period closed tonight." She got up from the swing. "Can I get you a beer?"

"Sure. Need some help?"

"No, I'm fine."

He watched as she crossed the porch to her front door and disappeared into the house. Her walk was smooth and graceful, the sway of her hips mesmerizing. *Oh, yeah. She's fine. Very fine indeed.*

When Shannon returned, she had a beer with a glass inverted over the bottle and another bottle similarly decorated. She handed him the beer before pouring herself what he now saw was mineral water and putting the bottle on the small wicker table in front of her.

"You're not joining me?"

"No, I don't drink alcohol." She sipped at her water but didn't break eye contact with him.

"That's right. You didn't have a glass of wine at dinner the other night either." Leo paused for a breath or two, wondering if he should ask. "Religious reasons?" He shook his head and tried to retract what he'd said. "Never mind. None of my business."

"I don't mind your asking. It's not religion, not in the way you mean, although I guess I'd define my mom as an avid believer in the church of alcohol. My father verges on being an alcoholic, too. I haven't seen him for a long time. He may be a full-blown one now for all I know." She paused, trying not to tear up remembering how long it had been since she'd seen him.

"Anyway, I decided not to begin down that path, in case it was in my genes."

"You should have said something. I don't need to have this." He gestured with the beer bottle. "I don't want you to be uncomfortable."

"Obviously I'm not. Otherwise I wouldn't keep beer and wine around for my friends. Please, enjoy it. I hear it's a really good IPA."

"Yup, it is. My favorite, in fact." He took a swig from the bottle. "Sounds like you're not too close to your family."

"Not really. My mom lives in Redding, California. I visit her three or four times a year and always come home sad because she's deteriorated a little bit more. She's never been here, which, in a lot of ways, is fine with me."

Shannon took another sip of her mineral water. "I'm not sure where my dad is. I think he's still in Reno. He left when I was young. Every now and then, he swoops in and plays daddy for a while, gives me advice on how to live my life, and makes promises he'll never keep. Then he leaves and I don't hear from him for another year or so." She sighed.

"Ever since I was a little girl, I've tried to get him to love me. I can't tell you how hard I worked to be the perfect daughter I thought he wanted me to be. But nothing has ever seemed to work. I don't know why I keep trying, but I do." Her eyes were bright with unshed tears.

"You want your father to care for you like all the rest of us do. But from what I can see, he's the one who's lost out by not being around you. You've done great with your life. With or without a relationship with him." Leo put his arm around her shoulders and gently urged her to put her head against his chest. "No brothers or sisters?"

"No, only me and mom." She sat up abruptly. "I don't know what's come over me. I didn't mean to turn this into a pity party. Sorry."

"You didn't. I asked." He leaned in and kissed her temple. "Don't run away."

She nestled back into his body. "What's your family like?"

"Like a three-ring circus most of the time. The rest of the time, meddling and nosy."

"In what way?" Shannon asked.

"Oh, you know, siblings with advice on how to live my life. Parents who worry about my choice of career because I don't have a 401k yet. The whole family wondering when I'm going to stop being the only unmarried one. The usual stuff."

"From the tone of your voice, you love them. Are they around here?"

"I do love them. To distraction. Yeah, they're in Portland. All of them. My mother and father are still in the house where I grew up out in Troutdale. My two brothers are an engineer and an accountant with the usual wives, kids, mortgaged homes, and dogs—which are not mortgaged, in case you were worried. One of my sisters is a police officer; the other is a librarian, both with the requisite spouses: wife in one case, husband in the other, along with kids and houses. No dogs. But there is a gerbil in the mix."

"Wow, big family. Where are you in the lineup?"

"I'm the youngest."

"Ah, so they fuss because you're the baby."

"Yes, and my parents are concerned because I'm the only one who didn't finish college so I don't have, as they keep reminding me, 'something to fall back on' if I need it."

"Which explains why this installation is so important to you, doesn't it?" Shannon asked.

"It's part of it. It could be the break I've been looking for. If I get some traction with the press, particularly the national media … " He let it trail off.

"You'll be on your way," she finished. "And I could have messed it up."

Leo pulled her closer to him with one arm and reached for the glass she was holding with his other hand. "Baby, you could never mess anything up for me." Her fingers trembled when he brushed them, and he heard her sharp intake of breath. She must have felt the same zing of electricity from their brief contact that he did.

Placing her glass on the table next to his beer bottle, he said, "You've made this a good thing regardless of how the glass installation turns out."

Those big eyes looking at him, the soft, pink lip she was biting almost undid him. He wanted to kiss her more than he'd ever wanted to kiss anyone. Had ever since the first day he'd met her. He kept reminding himself he wanted to take it slow, not rush in and get involved too fast, like he had with Cathy. But she didn't make it easy to keep his promise to himself.

Caressing her cheeks with the tips of his fingers elicited another gasp. Then she licked her lips. Just licked her lips and he had to fight the urge to cover her mouth and devour it with his own.

But, determined to take his time, he feathered kisses along her jawline. Light—butterfly light—kisses barely touching her skin but allowing him to taste her, tempt her, tease her.

"Leo, please," she pleaded as she moved her hands up his chest until her arms were wrapped around his neck and she was straining against him, her head back.

Instead of answering her plea, he kissed his way down her neck until he was at the base of her throat where he nipped at the soft flesh there, then bathed it with his tongue as if to heal whatever he may have hurt. God, she was sweet. Soft and sweet and smelling of spring.

Finally, Shannon took his face in her hand and said, "If you're not going to really kiss me, I'm going to kiss you."

Chapter Six

The mouth Leo locked on hers was hot and demanding. The arms he tightened around her were as strong and solid as she remembered from when he'd saved her from falling on the parade grounds. The heat of his body warmed up the cool spring night faster than any fire could. Shannon felt protected, sheltered, cared for, turned on. It had been so long since she'd been aroused like this. She'd almost forgotten how wonderful it felt. Leo's kiss was burning away her reluctance to let him get closer.

His mouth opened on hers and she responded, letting his tongue explore all the secrets of her mouth, playing with her tongue, the velvet slide of their game heating her more. All the breath in her lungs seemed to disappear into him as he swallowed her moan of pleasure.

She wanted to go where this kiss was leading them. From the way he fit her body to his, she knew he did, too. Her back arched and her head went back, hinting at her need to have him touch her breasts, to kiss the pulse in her throat. He immediately moved his mouth to the base of her throat. His hands went to the side of her breasts, barely touching her at first, then cupping her breasts from underneath, teasing at what they could do to arouse her more. Her arms around his neck tightened; her body responded to his with liquid heat. She wanted the kiss to go on and on. Wanted it to lead to what was next. Wanted him. Every way she could have him.

Suddenly, she felt cool air on her throat and his hands were gone. He'd pulled back from her, ducking his head, refusing to make eye contact.

She was confused. "Leo? Is something wrong?"

"I didn't mean for this to get out of hand so fast." She could tell he was working to bring his breathing back to normal. His heart hadn't gotten the message yet because it was pounding against her hands, now clutching at his shirt, trying to pull him back toward her.

"It didn't get out of hand. It was wonderful."

He took her face in his hands. "More than wonderful. But I can't tonight. I mean it's not possible. Walter's waiting."

"Who's Walter? Your father? A brother?" She paused as a thought struck her, before she realized she was being absurd. He kissed too convincingly for Walter to be *that* kind of friend. "Who is he? Why's he stopping us … stopping you? Can't you call him, text him, tell him you're staying?"

"Can't. Sorry."

Shannon wasn't exactly sure what to say so she said nothing, hoping her disappointment wasn't showing too much.

Leo continued. "His paws make it hard for him to answer the phone. And the instructor at obedience school didn't teach him to read a text."

"Paws? Obedience school?" Then what he meant dawned on her and she laughed. "Oh, Walter's your dog."

"He is. And he's been left alone for way too long. You can't imagine the damage he can do when he's pissed off at me. I apologize. I didn't think it would … didn't count on being … " He shook his head in frustration. "I don't know what I mean except I wasn't thinking before I started something I knew I couldn't finish."

"Don't apologize. I was the one who kissed you."

"Yeah, and I put up a whole hell of a lot of resistance, didn't I?"

"Well, now that you mention it … " She finished the sentence with a giggle.

He rose from the swing and put out his hand for her. "I better go before I forget how much glass he broke the last time he was annoyed with me. I don't have the time to clean up the mess he'd make." He gathered her into his arms when she stood. After he kissed her forehead he asked, "Can we pick up where we—where I—left off this weekend?"

Her head was against his chest where she could feel his heartbeat still racing. It pleased her and made her brave enough to say, "Why don't you bring Walter over here on Saturday? We can walk him around Vancouver and show him the sights. Then we can have dinner here." She paused for a moment then took a leap. "You both can stay for as long as you want."

"How about dinner tomorrow night and the walk on Saturday morning?"

"Or the whole weekend here?" She was grinning up at him by now.

"I'll bring his dog bed."

After Shannon had accompanied Leo to his truck and gotten one more scorching kiss, she returned home wondering how the hell she'd gotten the nerve to … well … to proposition him. Which was exactly what she'd done. Propositioned a man. She'd never done anything like it in her life. Maybe it was a mistake. Maybe she'd acted too quickly. No, it didn't feel like that at all. Right now, she felt like Leonardo DiCaprio on the prow of the Titanic. She was the king of the world. Okay, maybe the princess of Vancouver. But it felt good. Very good.

All she had to do was get through the night and work tomorrow and she'd have a sexy man in her house—in her bed—for the first time in a long, long time.

The sleeping part didn't work out too well—she was restless all night long. Then it was harder than she thought getting to the end of what felt like the longest workday in her life. Every time she checked her computer only ten or fifteen minutes had passed, although it didn't stop her from constantly looking. She tried all the tricks she knew to take her mind off the evening ahead, pulling up file after file of work-related subjects, hoping to lose herself in a complicated project but she couldn't. The only thing she could focus on was the list of vendors and artists to contact for the Fourth. At least she had done that and made all of them happy. She was Googling romantic dinner suggestions instead of eating lunch when she heard someone say her name in a frustrated tone. She looked up from her computer, hastily closing the webpage she'd been browsing. It was her best friend, Powell Jordan, who also worked in community relations.

"Hey there," Shannon said.

"Hey, yourself," Powell responded. "What's zoning you out so much I have to say your name three times before you answer? You must not be feeling well, because it's too much to ask to have you mooning over a guy."

"No, I'm not sick."

With her hands on her hips Powell asked the obvious question. "Then who is he?"

The question presented a problem. On one hand, telling her friend about Leo opened the door to hassle from her. On the other hand, if she didn't talk, Powell would bug her until she got the information she wanted. So, taking the path of least resistance, Shannon sighed and gave her friend the information she was after. "There is someone. A guy I met recently. A nice guy."

"It's about damn time. Spill. Who is he? How'd you meet him? Are you mooning about because tonight is the night for the doing of the deed or because it has already been done?"

Shannon went to the door of her cubicle and looked around to see who was in sight. "Keep your voice down! This isn't anybody else's business." She returned to her desk chair and waved Powell to another seat. "And I don't want it spread all over the office. Here's the thing. He's the glassblower I had to work with on the art project for the Fourth."

"The one you said was an airheaded PITA?"

"That one. But I was wrong. He's smart and sweet and sexy …"

"All the right S words so far. How about the big one—single?" Powell asked.

"That too."

"So deets ... now."

"Well, last week we had lunch one day, and over the weekend we went to the movies. He hung out at the house for a while last night. And I ... " Shannon paused, ducked her head and took a deep breath. "I asked him to spend the weekend with me."

"My, my, my. We've come a long way since Jeremy the Jackass left, haven't we?"

"It's time to get past him. Time to, I don't know, take a guy to bed and have fun. Not get all wrapped up in some relationship. Just have a good time." She giggled. "I've never done anything like this before. I don't know what got into me."

"Obviously the hope he would."

"*Powell!*"

Powell stood and motioned Shannon to do the same. "This calls for a quick trip to Van Mall. You haven't had lunch yet, have you?

"No, I was going to have a power bar at my desk. What's at Van Mall? There's no grocery store there. I was planning to go to Fred Meyer's after work."

"Honey, what you need isn't on sale at Freddy's. You need sexy undies, the kind that make a man go weak in the knees and hard a bit north of there."

"Do you have to make it sound like I'm some sort of slut? I'm not after him just for sex."

"If you're not after him for what those undies will tempt him to do, I'll be disappointed in you, sweet pea."

"I can't ... "

"You can. Grab your jacket. It's raining. We're going to see what secrets Victoria will let us in on."

After an hour and more money than Shannon had ever spent on underwear before, she had a lacy black bra and a matching pair of skimpy bikini panties. Powell wanted her to wear an uncomfortable looking thong that was also part of the line. Shannon finally bought it to shut her up but knew she'd return it as soon as she was out from under her friend's supervision.

The set of lingerie would, Powell assured her, get her through Friday evening. She then picked out a black silk kimono robe and a knit lounge set consisting of a cami and yoga pants to get her friend through the rest of the weekend. The lounge set was the only thing Shannon was sure she'd wear again. When she signed the credit card slip, she winced. But at least she was finished with her friend's meddling.

No such luck.

In the car on the way back to city hall, Powell asked, "What are you serving for dinner?"

"I thought I'd make steak and salad, with a baked potato and brownies. He's coming over at seven and I don't have a lot of time to fuss with something more complicated."

"The brownies are good. Chocolate is sexy. But the rest is boring. You need something more exciting, more romantic."

"I'm not doing oysters and champagne. Too obvious. And he'd have to drink the whole bottle of champagne." Shannon tried to sound as firm as she could.

"Right. It *is* too obvious and you don't want him drunk and unable to perform. But seafood is a good idea. How about cioppino? It's full of aphrodisiac tomatoes and spices, and has clams and mussels you can feed each other. It's easy to make and delicious. A nice loaf of bread. Wine or beer for him. Then those brownies."

"Sure you don't want to come by and check out my arrangements tonight? Maybe give me some advice on what I should do *after* dinner?" Shannon asked, trying hard not to let sarcasm completely take over her tone of voice.

"No," Powell said. "Not necessary. Even if you can't remember how to find your way around a man's body, if he's as hot as you say he is, he'll help you along."

"Oh, for God's sake, Powell. I may be younger than you are but I'm neither a virgin nor a prude. Give me some credit here."

"Okay, sweetie, okay. No need to go postal here. Only trying to make sure you have the weekend you've been needing ever since Jeremy the Jerk went AWOL."

Shannon laughed. "You know, I do deserve a good weekend. And I'm going to make sure Leo and Walter and I have one."

"Leo and Walter? You didn't tell me he was into ménage."

"It's his dog, Powell. Walter is a dog. Geesh. What a mind you have."

"Damn. I was hoping you'd introduce me when you got finished with them."

Chapter Seven

Shannon only had an hour and a half after she got home from the grocery store to get the sauce base for the cioppino going, the table set, and herself ready. After a quick shower, she got into the new bra and bikini panties which, she had to admit, looked great on her and made her feel sexy. What would cover the new undies took more time. She tried on a skirt, a dress, two pairs of pants, three shirts, and a sweater before deciding on a pair of black pants, a coppery-brown knit top, and a black and copper print scarf.

Her clothing indecision left her only a bit of time to fuss with the setting for her dinner with Leo. After cueing up her iPod with her favorite Decemberist album then setting the table with lots of candles and her best placemats, she make a swing through the living room, tidying up the already spotless room.

Her living room, with its off-white couch, Mission style rocking chair, and deep red Oriental knock-off area rug always looked neat. But she fluffed up a couple of red pillows on the couch, moved one book and a few magazines around on the low cocktail table in front of the couch, and realigned the angle of the table itself by one-half inch. Rearranging the books in the small bookshelf near the door, she began to have second thoughts. Maybe this hadn't been such a great idea. Was she really the kind of woman who asked a guy to spend the weekend? Used him for sex? That's what it felt like she was doing because she didn't think she was ready to get involved in any other way. Not with her track record.

Her swirling misgivings were interrupted by a knock on the door.

"Hi," Leo said before she could say anything. "Are we early?" He smelled freshly showered and was wearing jeans and a soft-looking white cotton shirt with thin blue stripes and epaulets on the shoulders.

"No, not at all. Welcome. Please. Come in." She knew she sounded stilted and formal but wasn't sure how to relax.

Fortunately Leo knew how to make it happen. Kissing her on the forehead between her eyebrows where she was sure she was frowning, he said, "I thought you might like this," and handed her what looked like a bottle of wine.

She read the label—not wine, a sparkling apple cider.

"It's from an artisan cider mill in Eastern Washington. They're really good at what they do, I'm told."

On tiptoes, she thanked him with a kiss on the cheek. "You're so sweet! Thank you."

"I didn't know if you'd discovered them yet and figured you'd enjoy it." A beautiful golden retriever pushed between them. "Oh, and this is … "

"Walter," she finished. She knelt, put the bottle on the floor and put out her hands, palm up, so he could sniff them. "Hi, boy. Aren't you pretty?" Stroking down his sides, she continued making friendly noises as the dog licked first her hands, then her face, his tail wagging and brushing against Leo's legs.

"I don't believe it," Leo said. "He's usually shy with strangers until he's been around them for a while. But he obviously has good taste in who he warms up to so fast."

"He recognizes a dog lover when he smells one." She stood up, bottle in hand, and headed for the kitchen. Walter followed her without waiting for a signal from his owner.

"Hey, Walter. Remember me? The guy who pays your vet bills?" Leo said as he trailed after his dog.

"He must know I have a treat for him," Shannon said as she pulled a biscuit from a paper bag and fed it to him. "There's this great bakery in downtown, Bleu Door. They make wonderful bread and bake dog biscuits, too. I got some for him when I got bread for our dinner."

"He'll never go home with me now."

"I doubt he's so fickle." Shannon opened the refrigerator door and brought out a beer.

"He follows his stomach." Leo took the beer, shook his head at the proffered glass, and twisted off the cap. "Actually, so do I. And something smells good in here."

"It's cioppino." A panicky feeling swept over her. "Oh, my God, I never thought to ask. You're not allergic to shellfish, are you? Or are you vegan? Gluten sensitive? Anti-GMO?" She took a breath and was about to say, "Lactose intolerant?" when he interrupted.

"No. No. No and no. Do you quiz all your dinner guests this way?"

"Only the ones from Portland." She gave him a smile she hoped was innocent looking, even if the remark wasn't.

"Well, us guys from Troutdale aren't so fussy. You can stop looking like you're about to have a panic attack." His smile in return wasn't at all innocent, which made her quite happy.

•••

A couple hours later, they'd finished the cioppino and bread, eaten almost all of the salad, and in dinner table conversation, had found out more about each other. Shannon learned the college he didn't finish was Stanford, which he left after almost three years to work with the glassblowers at Firehouse Glass in Vancouver. A year later, he had the chance to move into the GlassCo studio owned by Amanda St. Claire, the well-known glass artist. Amanda had so much confidence in Leo and his work, she'd fronted the money for him to start on his July Fourth project before the grant had been processed from the Community Foundation. Yet another reason for him to want it to go well.

In turn, Shannon told him about her long, slow slog for a master's degree in public administration, which, she said, would take her into the next millennium at the rate she was going. They talked about movies and e-readers versus paper books. He told her about his studio mates and his friends at Firehouse Glass, and she told him about Powell, even admitted Powell had helped her plan the evening because she was afraid Shannon was out of practice.

Which, of course, led to a conversation about why she was out of practice. They were amused to discover her "I need more space" breakup had occurred at about the same time as Leo's "It's not you, it's me" breakup. However, it wasn't amusing enough to continue the discussion for very long and have exes get in the way of the rest of the evening.

Shannon cleared the table of their dinner dishes and was loading plates into the dishwasher when Leo followed her to the kitchen, came up behind her, and slid his hands around her waist.

"The dishes can wait, can't they? Let's take the plate of brownies into the living room." He began to nibble on her neck. "Yum. You taste as good as dinner did." He turned her around and pulled her against him. Lowering his head, he claimed her mouth in a blazing hot kiss, reminding her exactly how much he wanted her. She wanted to respond the same way, let him know she wanted him, too. But she was overcome with a sudden unexplained reluctance. Maybe it was their conversation over dinner touching on Jeremy. If it was, this was a fine time for him to rear his ugly head. She'd been over Jeremy for months. Maybe it was her head telling her heart not to get involved so she got hurt again.

More likely, her hesitancy was simpler than that: she was at the crucial point of what she'd set in motion the night before. Her courage was leaving on a jet plane and she didn't know when it would be back again.

He must have sensed it because he broke from the kiss and cocked his head, a slight frown on his handsome face. "Are you okay? Was it too much talk about our exes?"

She shook her head. "I don't know what's wrong with me. I was the one who asked you to stay for the weekend. And I planned the whole evening, even bought new underwear to impress you, but all of a sudden I feel shy."

It looked like he was trying hard not to smile. "New underwear, huh? Sounds like a pretty serious commitment to spending the weekend in bed."

She frowned, squinting her eyes. "Are you making fun of me?"

"Baby, I would never jeopardize my chances of seeing your new underwear by laughing at you." He squinted back at her. "Although you have to admit, it *is* close to being funny."

"You better kiss me again before I overthink this any more than I already have."

He was happy to oblige. This time the kiss was slow and sweet, his lips soft, his tongue lazy as it swept through her mouth. The evidence of his arousal pressed against her, making her response to his kisses even more intense as her body went along for the ride.

She sighed in his arms. "I have about three more dishes to put in the dishwasher, and you need to get Walter's dog bed and your things. Then we can get him settled and go … we can finish up … we can have dessert."

When Walter had been walked, fed, and settled with a chew toy in his bed, Leo joined her in the living room where she was sitting on the couch, playing with the brownie crumbs on her plate. He picked up a brownie and watched her as he took a bite. "You're nervous."

"It's obvious, isn't it? I've used up all my courage asking you to stay the weekend. And now, I'm not sure what's next. I've never propositioned a man before. What do I do now? Like, should I carry you upstairs or something?"

The trying-to-contain-a-laugh look returned. "I don't want to cast doubt on your abilities, but I don't think that's a good idea. It's not likely to result in anything other than one or both of us getting hurt, which would seriously interfere with what I had in mind for this evening. How about you lead me to your bedroom and I'll take it from there?"

"Oh, thank you." She was sure he could see her whole body relax with the relief she felt.

They may have been joking around downstairs, but once they were in her bedroom, all vestiges of humor disappeared when he turned out the overhead light she had flipped on.

"What are you doing?"

"Making it easier for you to let me finish up the seducing. This light's enough." He switched on a small light on her bedside table, which cast a warm, soft glow on the room.

Then his hands were on either side of her face, gentle, tender, caressing her with the pads of his thumbs. As he stroked her mouth, she sighed, her lips parted, and he teased her tongue with one thumb. She instinctively sucked on it and heard an answering groan from him.

He slid his hands slowly from her mouth to her neck to her shoulders as he feathered tiny kisses along her jawline. "I think it's time I get to see your new underwear," he whispered. Before she could agree, he was tugging on the hem of her sweater, bringing it up over her head, then tossing it on the floor.

The dark desire in his eyes when he saw the black bra barely covering her breasts made the torture of shopping with Powell worth it.

"Jesus, Shannon, you're beautiful." He fell to his knees, massaging one breast and cupping the other so he could take it into his mouth, scrape gently at the nipple through the lace, suck and lick it before he finally unhooked the front clasp and peeled off the bra. Returning his attention to her breasts when it was gone, his hot, wet, needy mouth now had no barrier between it and her sensitive nipples.

All her senses were concentrated on the connection between them. There was nothing in the world for her but the sensation he was creating. Then the tingle began to spread from her breast to her belly, from there to her core. Her knees became so wobbly, she didn't know how long she would be able to stand.

Leo must have somehow known because just before she reached the point of falling, he lay her down on the bed, pulled off her shoes, and unzipped and removed her pants. Clad now only in the black bikini panties and the flush of desire she could feel on her face, she was tempted to cover her breasts with her hands. But the look on his face, the desire in his eyes, made her want to show this gorgeous man, who wanted her as much as she wanted him, she was as brave as her words last night had been.

• • •

Unbuttoning the cuffs of his shirt, Leo didn't take his eyes off her. Her hair looked like honey spread out on the pillow, the way he'd imagined it. Her brown eyes were wide with desire, her pale pink nipples tight with arousal. If he said it every minute from now until hell froze over, he could never tell her enough how beautiful she was.

His shirt joined the pile of her clothes on the floor and so did his shoes. But the sight of her sprawled on the bed was irresistible. He couldn't finish undressing without kissing her again. Kneeling on the bed between her legs, he kissed his way up her body from the lacy band of her bikinis to her navel. From the valley between her breasts until he finally reached the base of her throat. He kissed, nipped, and sucked at her pulse point, feeling the pounding of her heart matching the rhythm of his.

When he sat up to finish undressing, Shannon beat him to the snap at the top of his jeans. And when she followed by lowering the zipper and taking him in her hand, he took in a surprised breath. The feel of her soft hand on his hard cock almost undid him. He groaned then reluctantly took her hand away.

"Let me get these off," he said. He shed the jeans and boxers after removing a condom from the pocket and placing it on the bedside stand. Returning to her, he reached for her hands and laced their fingers together.

"I want to go slow and easy. We're in no hurry tonight. I want to touch every inch of your skin, taste every bit of you."

She arched against him, breathing raggedly. "Yes. Please. Touch me." She guided one of their joined hands down between her legs. Even through her panties he could feel how wet she was already. He unlaced his fingers from hers and slid them under her panties. "We need to get rid of these." She lifted her hips, and the last barrier between them was gone.

His fingers could now range freely over her sex, parting the folds, finding the nub of her clitoris. "I love how wet you are for me," he whispered as he slid one finger into her core then a second one, massaging, caressing, making her cry out in pleasure before adding his thumb circling her clitoris until she called his name as she climaxed.

• • •

Shannon had never come so fast in her life. So fast and so spectacularly. She didn't know what else he had in mind for seducing her, but what he'd done so far was beyond anything she'd ever experienced. She was unable to move for the moment, overwhelmed by the strength of her climax.

"You okay, baby?" Leo had pulled her to him and was stroking her hair.

"Okay doesn't begin to cover it," she said in a whispery voice.

"And we have all night."

"We have all weekend," she said as she turned into him and began to nibble at his mouth with little love bites, tasting chocolate and what she thought must be beer, a delicious combination that she'd always remember as *Leo*. "It's your turn, though."

She could feel him smile against her mouth. "I'm doing just fine."

"I think we can make it better." She slid her hand down his ripped abs and flat belly to his penis. "I need to make good on my propositioning, don't you think?" His erection was steely except for the velvety soft tip where a few wet drops lubricated her hand as she massaged him. He grew even harder, bigger under her hand.

As she caressed and rubbed him, she trailed kisses down his jawline and the side of his neck. He groaned and pushed his hips forward, moving into her hand. She rubbed harder, as aroused by what she was doing to him and the reaction she was getting as she had been when he had been touching her.

But as she was about to straddle him so she could replace her hand with her body, he flipped her onto her back and grabbed the condom from the table. Ripping open the package, he said, "Here, cover me," his voice raspy with want.

She was sure her hands were shaking as she pinched the tip then unrolled the condom over him. When she was finished, she drew him between her legs and felt his hard length against her sex.

Bracing himself on his forearms Leo guided his penis into her, thrusting deep and strong, moving the electricity of their kissing and touching inside her. She could feel nothing but Leo on her, in her, around her. When he nuzzled her neck then moved to her mouth to add the rhythm of his tongue playing with hers to the feeling of his penis inside her, she gave herself completely to the sensation, the wonder of their bodies moving together, higher and higher, closer to another orgasm.

He increased the intensity of his thrusts and Shannon felt her own body respond with a rhythmic release, until they both dissolved into a climax leaving them breathless, sated, and silent.

Eventually, he broke the silence. Stroking her cheek he said, "I think this is where I thank you for the new underwear."

"You barely looked at it."

"Didn't have to study it for long to see it was covering a very sexy lady."

"I'm not sure a lady would wear black lace lingerie, but I'll tell Powell you appreciated it." She snuggled into his chest. "I have more for tomorrow. Not quite so minimal but still kinda sexy."

"Hmm. This is shaping up to be the best weekend I've had in forever." He kissed her on the forehead.

"Same for me." She looked up at his brilliant blue eyes. "I've never met a man like you before."

"Is it a good thing or a bad thing?" He was grinning now.

"It's a very good thing." She returned to snuggling against his chest. The silence returned as she drifted off to sleep.

Chapter Eight

In Shannon's dream she could hear an odd thumping sound as something wet and warm caressed her hand. She shook it off, but whatever it was, moved to her arm. It wasn't unpleasant. It was, however, weird. Finally she opened her eyes.

No dream. Walter was sitting beside her, licking her as his wagging tail hit the floor.

She groaned. "Walter, Leo's on the other side."

In a sleepy voice Leo said, "He wants out. I'm sorry he decided to ask you."

"It's what I get for feeding him treats last night. Go find Leo, Walter." The dog didn't move.

By the time she turned toward him, Leo had put on his jeans and was tying his shoes. "I'll take him out and be right back."

She sat up, holding the sheet over her breasts. "I'll make coffee while you're gone."

The grin he aimed at her was the most wicked thing she'd ever seen. "Stay right where you are. I have plans for how I want to start the morning. And they don't include coffee quite yet." He made a clicking noise and Walter came to his side. "And I've already seen your beautiful breasts. You don't have to hide them."

She dozed off again so she wasn't sure how long he was gone. All she knew was the next time she woke it was to a much nicer sensation than having her hand licked. Her body was being stroked. It was sensuous, seriously sexy. Leo was spooned around her back, one arm somehow under her neck and the other around her waist. The beginning of an erection was pressed against her bottom; his hand was busy bringing her nipples to hard peaks.

"Mmm. Feels good. I like waking up to you better than to Walter," she said as she rolled over to face him.

"I hope so. I'd hate to be in second place behind my dog."

"You said something about plans?" She rubbed her fingertips over his morning stubble.

"Yeah. I thought we'd start with a little of this." He kissed her gently, his lips soft and satisfying, at the same time making her want more. He gave it to her with tiny nips to her mouth and quick little licks with his tongue. "Then, maybe this." His hand returned to her breast, stroking, massaging, finishing the task of bringing her nipples to hard, pebbly points.

"Would it upset your plans if I added this?" she asked as she reached between them to stroke his penis, feeling it harden under her touch.

He groaned his approval before taking possession of her mouth again, tangling his tongue with hers in a kiss now moving from sweet all the way to sexy.

"Condom," she managed to say in a raspy, breathless voice. She heard the rip of the packet behind her back and then it was in her hand.

She quickly covered him and was about to lie on her back when he pulled her leg up over his hip and entered her.

• • •

Although it was only the second time they'd made love, it felt like he'd found the place he belonged. Shannon was so receptive, so passionate in her response. Leo couldn't imagine anyone being more in tune with him.

He wanted this to last, as he had the night before, but the taste of her mouth, the smell of her skin when she was aroused, the slip and slide of their bodies moving on mingled sweat, the feel of her inner muscles already beginning to pull at him were more than he could fight. With one last deep thrust he poured himself into her as they found their release together.

He touched his forehead to hers then kissed her there. "So, how'd you like the plan for starting the morning?"

A soft breathy laugh cooled his neck. "You're a marvelous planner. You should work for the city. We'd all have a lot more fun if you made plans like this for us every day."

"Thanks for the offer but there's only one person in city hall I want to plan for and she's right here." He skimmed his hand down her side.

"You don't have to flatter me, Leo. We're just having fun."

"I'm not flattering you; it's true." He kissed her forehead again before he sat up. "It's also true I'm hungry. Let's go someplace and eat. I've heard for years about Tommy O's great breakfasts but I've never been there."

"I have eggs and turkey sausage and fresh orange juice and morning buns ..."

"You fed us last night. It's my turn."

"Nope. It was my idea to spend the weekend here so it's still my turn." She jumped out of bed. "Dibs on the first shower."

Half an hour later, both of them had showered and were in fresh clothes and had made their way to the kitchen. They were finding their rhythm there as Leo fed Walter, then made coffee, and Shannon fried the sausage patties and eggs. When it was all put together, they ate, the comfortable camaraderie of the table from the night before still evident in their conversation.

Breakfast finished, the dishes done, and the coffee pot empty, Shannon said, "So what's the planner got in mind for the day?" In response to his smirk, she said, "Other than the obvious."

"There was a promise of a walking tour of Vancouver for Walter and me."

"Let's do it, then. I think Walter would like to see some of our public art, don't you?"

"Definitely. Walter's really into public art."

• • •

The three of them—Leo, Shannon, and Walter, one of them on a leash, two of them holding hands—started west, across the I-5 overpass, heading to Esther Short Park. Along the way Shannon pointed out the tower of brightly colored metallic umbrellas on Main Street, one of the latest additions to the city's collection of public art, and he asked to see the child with the glass balloons his friends at Firehouse had worked on.

Leo had already seen the park's clock tower and water feature with the salmon running when they'd had lunch outside a couple weeks before so Shannon led him to the pioneer mother statue, one of the city's oldest pieces of public art. He did point out she was facing north, which made her seem a little lost, unlike the pioneers in front of the Justice Center in Portland who were frozen in place perpetually facing west, their goal from the day they left their homes in the east. Shannon suggested the pioneers in the park here might have realized they'd taken a wrong turn and this wasn't Vancouver, Canada, and re-aimed their sights north.

The tour continued past the statue of Captain Vancouver for whom the city was named, although only his statue and not the man himself had ever been in the area. From there they went toward the Columbia River, past the Boat of Discovery, which commemorated the exploration of the area.

He loved her enthusiasm for her city and told her.

"You haven't seen the best yet. I've saved it for last and then we can head home."

Leo looked around the area where Shannon had led them but saw nothing more than trees, two restaurants, and an assortment of parking lots. "I'm not sure I look at cars, a road, and an embankment with railroad tracks on top as art."

"The berm for the tracks hides what I want you to see," she said as she continued to walk, "but there's an entrance right … " She pointed to an opening. "Right there."

Before Leo could say anything, Walter went after another dog ahead of them and pulled Shannon, who was holding his leash, onto the north side of the berm. Leo jogged to catch up.

"Before we go any further, you have to give obeisance to the Old Apple Tree," Shannon said. "According to legend, John McLoughlin planted the tree when he was living here and in charge of the Hudson's Bay Company. It's well over 150 years old and may be the oldest apple tree in the west."

Leo bowed to the tree. "I always respect my elders. But even if it's impressive for a tree to live so long, it's not public art."

"Look to your right," Shannon ordered.

What Leo saw when he did was a two-story cedar log gate topped with crossed canoe paddles and what appeared to be a silvery glass mask. Beyond it was a wide, paved path curving around and up, leading to something not completely visible. "It's beautiful but what is it?"

"It's the entry to the Land Bridge. The Confluence Project built it. It's one of seven art installations along the Columbia River interpreting the intersection of environment, culture, and history. It's my favorite piece of public art. Come on, let me show you the rest."

"Wait, I want to look at the mask."

"Lillian Pitt did it."

"I've seen her clay and mixed media pieces, but I didn't know she did glass." Leo pulled out his phone and took a picture of the gate, then called Shannon's name to get her to turn around so he could capture an image of her with Walter.

"Did I look as dorky as I felt?" she asked.

"Oh, did I take a photo of you? I was going for a photo of Walter. Can't have too many pictures of your pet, can you?"

She shook her head. "Yeah, right. Okay, if you won't tell me how dorky I looked, let's walk up to the top. I want you to see the metal sculpture baskets Lillian Pitt did for the bridge itself."

"So, what's the story about this? If it's your favorite, you must know a lot about it."

She did. And she told him all of it as they walked up the ramp to the top of the bridge crossing over Highway 14. Covered in native grasses and plants, it represented the prairie lifted up over the road, reconnecting the Fort Vancouver site with the Columbia River. The site was part of the old Klickitat Trail, a meeting place for Native Americans long before Lewis and Clark arrived or the Hudson's Bay Company laid claim to the land.

"But after the art, my favorite part," she said, as they arrived at the overlook on the south side, "is this." Her grand gesture showed off what must be, Leo thought, the best view in Vancouver.

To the south was the Columbia River, which formed the northern border of both Oregon and the city of Portland. To the west lay the I-5 Bridge and the downtown core of Vancouver. To the east, situated at what appeared to be the end of the river, was Mount Hood, still clad in winter snow.

Even Walter seemed to understand this wasn't a moment for running after other dogs. He sat quietly at Shannon's feet.

Leo put his arm around Shannon's shoulders. "This is amazing. I heard about it on the local news when it was dedicated but I never thought to come here."

"Like I said, it's my favorite place in Vancouver." She smiled up at him. "I'm happy you like it."

As they walked over the bridge to the grounds of Fort Vancouver, Walter re-met the dog he had briefly chased on the south side. He was a mastiff and Walter was much more interested in him than he was in Walter. In fact, Arno—his owner introduced him—hid, tail between his legs, behind his mistress. He was, she explained, more a Ferdinand the Bull animal than the furry monster he appeared to be. Walter walked away from the encounter looking quite cocky about his intimidation of a larger dog.

He also seemed happy with the rest of the day. Shannon and Leo tossed a ball for him on the parade grounds in front of her home and followed him around while he chased squirrels. When they'd worn him out—or vice versa—they took him back to Shannon's house where they cooked dinner together before going to a midnight show of an old movie at the Kiggins Theater so Leo could see the renovations in the Art Deco-style theater. On Sunday they went to the restaurant Leo had heard about for breakfast.

Oh, and they made love. Any chance they got.

Chapter Nine

Monday morning's staff meeting was the usual—Randy Andy venting at his staff in his normal management-by-intimidation style. This Monday, however, Shannon really didn't care who said what to whom. She was still on a cloud of … something. She didn't want to analyze it; she wanted to enjoy it.

However, when her boss asked her to stay after everyone else was dismissed, she knew she had little chance to make her good mood last.

With a slight smirk on his face, he began with, "So, I hear you've worked things out with our star artist."

Shannon had a minute of panic. Had Larson heard somehow about her weekend with Leo? Where was he headed with this?

"I'm not sure I understand."

"Worked it out. You got the permits and permissions taken care of and he signed off. What do you think I meant?"

"Yes, I have everything signed and filed with the appropriate departments."

The smirk disappeared to be replaced with an expression Shannon knew meant he was about to rip into her. "It's about time. I have to say, Ms. Morgan, I've been disappointed in your performance since you moved to my department. You've certainly not lived up to the hype I heard from the mayor's office when they recommended you. Or were they trying to prune dead wood by sloughing you off on me?"

Shannon took a few seconds to compose herself before she answered. Her automatic response was to tell him to get stuffed—or worse. But she knew she would only inflame the situation. Which, she suspected, was exactly what Larson was counting on.

"I'm sorry you're disappointed in my work. I've tried to uphold the standards of the department."

"Well, you haven't succeeded. And if you don't pull it together over the Independence Day event, you may find yourself outside looking in." He handed her a sheaf of papers; in them, she noticed, were phone calls unanswered for days. "Take care of this. They're mostly from potential vendors. We make money off the vendors. They're important."

Then why didn't you give me these phone messages when you got them? Oh, wait, because then you'd have nothing to harass me about.

"I will." She stuffed the papers into her notebook. "Anything else?"

"No, I think I've covered it. But make no mistake, I'm watching you."

Like a hawk watches prey. But I'm not going to let you have me for lunch, buddy.

She left the conference room with her head held high, determined to get back the good mood her weekend had put her in.

Less than five minutes later, Powell showed up at the door to her cubicle, which was even less of a surprise than her conversation with her boss had been.

"So what did Randy Andy want?" her friend began.

"The usual. I'm not living up to expectations. I better straighten up or I'm gone. Nothing new."

"Didn't he know you got the art installation taken care of?"

"Yes, but not the vendor phone calls he hadn't given me yet." Shannon showed her the stack of phone messages.

"Son of a bitch. He'd do anything to make you look bad, wouldn't he?"

"Yeah, and ruin my morning when I was feeling pretty good."

"I'd say more than pretty good. You have the look of a woman who has been well and truly fucked," Powell said. She plopped down in the chair across from Shannon's desk. "My weekend felt like one long meditative session with Buddhist monks—silent, celibate, and boring. Let me live vicariously, please. I need specifics."

"Powell, can you keep it under the decibel level of a fighter jet, please? I'm not interested in having my social life spread all over the office like peanut butter."

"Social life? Who cares about your social life? I want to know about your sex life, since you actually have one now." She leaned across the desk. "On the time-honored scale of one to ten, with one being the worst sex you've ever had and ten the best, where did the weekend rank?"

"About twenty."

"Oh, my God, I am drooling here. He's that good?"

"I don't know what your criteria are … "

"How many times did you come?"

"It would be oversharing to tell, Powell."

"You asked what my standards are. I told you."

Shannon made a shooing motion. "Begone, woman. I have to get some work done today."

"When do you see Studly-Do-Right again?"

"We're spending next weekend in Portland at his place. He said it'll take him a week to get it cleaned up enough to allow me to see it."

"The man cleans, too? Honey, you've got hold of a real gem."

Two minutes of talking with Powell about her weekend and her good mood made a rapid return. She went back to her work with renewed energy and tore through her to-do list, making the phone calls her boss had given her to answer, handling emails, and drafting the minutes from her meetings the previous week. She even managed to soothe a couple angry phone callers about parking fines.

The day flew by. She was about to wrap things up so she could leave for home when she glanced up from the desk. A man was standing in the doorway to her cubicle. The good feeling disappeared again; this time she was afraid it was permanent.

"What are you doing here?" she asked. She could feel her shoulders tighten and her throat clench.

"I came by to see if you'll have a glass of wine with me after work," her ex-boyfriend Jeremy Vincent said. "I need to talk to you." He'd lost weight since she'd last seen him. He was leaner, tougher looking. And he had a tan so dark his skin looked like aged leather.

"You know I don't drink. And what do we have to talk about? You left. I stayed. That about says it all."

"It's important, Shannon. I know I wasn't fair to you when I left. I want to start over, do it right this time."

"Just like that, I'm supposed to pick up where we left off when I haven't heard from you in a year?" She grabbed her messenger bag and rain jacket. "I don't think so, Jeremy." She tried to move past him but he blocked the doorway. "Do I need to call security and have them remove you from the building?" she asked.

"Is this how you treat the citizens of the city of Vancouver?"

"Don't worry about it. You don't live in Vancouver."

"Yes I do. I moved from Portland so I can be close to you. To make it up to you for what I did to hurt you."

"You've got one hell of an ego. But don't worry. You're off the hook. I'm fine. Except I can't get out of my office to go home."

"I learned a lot about myself spending all that time alone. I learned we belong together, Shannon. Haven't you always felt that, too?"

"Are you okay, Shannon?" Powell's voice cut into the conversation. "Do you need security?" She was standing directly behind Jeremy, her cell phone in her hand. The expression on her face would have made a boulder disintegrate into gravel.

"No, thanks, Powell. Jeremy was leaving, weren't you?"

Jeremy hesitated for a moment but, bookended by two women who seemed determined to face him down, he finally moved. "I'll leave. But I'm not giving up. I know now what I need. You. And I won't stop trying to convince you I mean it. No matter what it takes." He strode toward the elevator leaving the two women to gape after him.

"What the hell is he talking about?" Powell asked.

"Apparently he believes I suffered when he left, and he's graciously offered to make up for it," Shannon said. "I'm not sure what to do about it. Maybe I should sit down and talk to him, just to clear the air."

"Or maybe you need a restraining order."

"Like for stalkers?"

"Yes. If he won't go away that's exactly what he is."

Shannon shuddered, knowing what Powell had gone through a couple years before. The story she'd told about black eyes and sprained wrists, slashed tires, and break-ins was horrific. In Powell's case, it had been her ex-husband. It had required the intervention of law enforcement, and when the police couldn't stop him, a move from Colorado to Washington State to get away from him. "This is nothing like that. He caught me off balance, that's all. I don't think he's dangerous. More like annoying. Actually, I kinda feel sorry for him. He looked so pathetic."

"He was standing too close to you and he sounded way too demanding. You need to watch your back, Shannon. From what I heard of the conversation, I don't trust him." Powell grinned at her friend. "On the other hand, maybe you can find someone who'll want to watch your back for you. Maybe a guy who's hot and sexy. Know anyone like that?"

All the way home, Shannon thought about Powell's advice. A restraining order. It sounded like something out of *Law and Order: SVU*. She didn't think it was necessary. But then, she would never have thought she'd see Jeremy again much less have him suddenly appear and ask to get back together.

She didn't understand her ex. When they were together he'd hardly thought they were the soul mates of romance novels. She didn't think forever had been on the table for either of them. Granted, her father had met him once, and on the basis of a short acquaintance, seemed to assume he was the one for her. But no one else did.

No question she'd been hurt when he left, but that was as much because of the way he left than anything else. He'd disappeared while she was at work one day, leaving no trace, not taking the few things he'd left at her house. He hadn't even left a note. It scared the bejesus out of her worrying about him until he texted her a few days later to say he needed space and was off to hike the Pacific Crest Trail. He explained it wasn't her; it was him. He'd been rude; he'd scared her, and she had to admit, her pride had been dinged a bit by the way he'd ended things. More than anything, he'd confirmed what she'd always thought anyway—she had lousy luck in dealing with the opposite sex.

Maybe though, for the sake of closure, she should see him again. Not to revive what she was sure was no longer there, but to put it firmly in her past. She made herself smile when the thought occurred she could thank him for leaving in such a way that she was angry at all the males on the planet, making her unattached when Leo came along.

On the other hand, if Powell was right, if she'd seen something Shannon had missed in Jeremy, if he was capable of doing something like stalking, maybe encouraging him wasn't such a good idea. Shannon tried to get the idea of being stalked out of her mind, but she couldn't. Powell had spooked her.

Her friend's warning stayed with her as she fixed and then ate dinner, while she loaded the dishwasher with her breakfast and dinner dishes. She tried to settle in her living room with a book, but she couldn't concentrate. Every sound—and the old building she lived in made lots of creaky noises—made her think someone was outside on the porch, at her back door. She jumped at the wind, started when the rain changed directions, read the same page five times interrupted by the groans and moans of the house or by her neighbors making noises. At the rate she was going, she wouldn't get much sleep. Something had to be done or she'd be a total mess by morning.

She wished she had a dog. Walter would have been good company tonight. Wait. That's what she needed—company. She started to call Powell but couldn't push the button to ring her. If Powell came over, she'd make her more nervous about Jeremy being a stalker and she needed someone to tamp down the feeling, not make it worse. Then she had an idea. Walter's owner.

Leo answered on the second ring. "Hey, Shannon. What's up?"

"Nothing. I needed to … wanted to … thought maybe we could talk."

Leo paused for a moment before asking, "Are you okay? You sound, I don't know, different. Upset maybe."

"No, I'm fine."

"You sure?"

"Well, maybe not exactly fine." She was silent for a bit, trying to find the words to explain why she was freaking out. "Jeremy, my ex-boyfriend, came to my office to ask me to have a drink with him."

"He didn't remember you don't drink?"

"I guess not. I don't know. That's not the point, though. He's back in town and he's discovered what he needs from life. Me. He wants us to get back together."

Chapter Ten

What the fuck? Get back together with her old boyfriend? Leo heard the words but didn't want to believe them. She couldn't, could she? Or could she, and the tense, upset tone of her voice was because she was going to tell him so?

He hesitated for a moment before saying, "Okay. He wants to get back together. What do *you* want?"

"I don't want to get back with him, but I kinda feel bad about the way I ran him out of my office today. He's not a bad person. Although Powell says she doesn't trust him. She told me to get a restraining order because she thought he was verging on being a stalker. She scared me more than he did."

Leo exhaled the breath he didn't realize he'd been holding before saying, "Walter and I are on our way."

"You don't have to come over here. I'll be fine. Just talk to me."

"You're not fine, and you need some company. We'll be there in fifteen minutes."

Leo didn't register how relieved he was Shannon wasn't interested in her ex until he had loaded Walter into his truck and was on I-5 headed for Vancouver. It took that long for his shoulders to slump back into their natural position and the muscle at the back of his neck to let go of the knot he'd felt appear when Shannon told him her ex wanted her back.

He'd thought about her a lot since their weekend together. Her intelligence and sense of humor. Her eye for art and her enthusiasm for her city. The way she loved Walter and how Walter loved her. The fireworks he created with her in bed.

He'd already planned out the coming weekend. And the one after, and the one after, on into the summer. Not to mention looking forward to working on the installation for the Fourth together.

None of what he planned included an ex-boyfriend hanging around.

When Shannon opened her front door, he could see on her face the strain he'd heard in her voice. "Jesus, baby, you look so worried." He took her in his arms and held her until he felt her relax against him.

"I shouldn't have let you do this, but I'm so glad you're here." She sounded like she was on the edge of tears, holding on by a thin thread.

"Let's sit down. Tell me about it."

She sat in Leo's arms with Walter's head on her thigh while she related the story of Jeremy's unexpected visit. By the time she'd finished, she was noticeably more relaxed.

Until the doorbell rang and she startled at the sound.

"Are you expecting someone?" Leo asked.

"No." She stood to go to the door but he stopped her.

"Walter and I will get it. You stay here."

It was a man, a bit shorter and younger than he was, tan, fit looking. "Can I help you?" Leo said.

"Sorry I must have the wrong place. I was looking for Shannon Morgan. I guess she moved."

"Who's looking for her?"

"I'm an old friend, Jeremy Vincent."

"You're her ex-boyfriend and she doesn't want to see you."

"Oh, then you know her." He looked past Leo, searching the room for Shannon. "And she's here, isn't she?"

"She doesn't want to see you," Leo repeated.

"You're mistaken. I hurt her when I left on my vision quest, and I want to make it up to her. You can't keep me from seeing her." Jeremy began to push his way into the house but was stopped by a growl from Walter.

"Even my dog knows she doesn't want to see you," Leo said. "Leave before I call the police."

Jeremy stepped back out of range of Walter's mouth. "Shannon," he yelled, "I'll be back. I have to see you."

Leo slammed the door and threw the deadbolt.

Shannon was shaking when he sat down next to her. "I don't know what to do," she said. "Do you really think he'll turn into a stalker?"

"I don't know, baby, but I think you better be extra cautious for a while until you can figure it out." He stroked her hair and kissed the top of her head. "You can come stay with Walter and me if you'd like."

"Let me think about it."

"Don't wait too long. I don't know him well enough to know if he's a threat, but I do know you're upset by it and I don't like to see you like this." He took his arm from around her. "Why don't I make you a cup of tea while you stay here with Walter?"

"Yes, please. There are some chamomile teabags in the cupboard to the left of the sink."

A short time later, Leo brought two steaming mugs to the living room.

After finishing most of her tea, Shannon put the mug on the coffee table. She yawned. "It must be working already." She yawned again. "All of a sudden I'm awfully tired."

"Adrenaline let down. Let's get you to bed." Before she could say what he was sure she was thinking, he added. "To go to sleep, nothing more. I'll stay until I'm sure you're asleep and then Walter and I'll leave."

"Thank you, Leo. A friend like you is what I needed tonight."

He finally learned what she wore to bed when he wasn't there—a cute little tank top and pajama bottoms that hung from her hips. Too bad sleep was the only thing on the agenda for the night. She looked sexy as hell. But sleep was what she needed, so he lay beside her on top of the comforter, fully clothed, rubbing her back until she drifted off.

On his way home, what she said finally made its way into his consciousness. Friends? She thought they were friends? He already knew he wanted more. The question was, did she? And if she was reluctant, what could he do to convince her it was okay to want more, too?

• • •

Shannon woke to a bright shiny object in the sky, something she hadn't seen in days. The sunshine pouring down elevated her mood considerably. In the light of day, Jeremy didn't seem like much of a problem after all. Leo and Walter had made the point she'd moved on, had someone else in her life, and didn't want to see him. Surely Jeremy understood and would back off. She had let the sudden appearance of her ex and Powell's dire warnings make her jumpy. There was nothing to be afraid of.

Powell, of course, was waiting for her when she got to work. Shannon reassured her, saying everything was fine. Leo had run Jeremy off. Powell allowed as how Studly-Do-Right got better and better with each passing day. Shannon had to agree.

There was nothing more from Jeremy until Friday when a bouquet of flowers was delivered to her office. The accompanying note apologized and asked for a chance to start over. He called an hour after the flowers were delivered, but she was in a meeting. He left a message on her voice mail with his new phone number.

Shannon donated the flowers to a colleague who was having a birthday party for his wife on Saturday and ignored the request to call back. Even if she'd wanted to talk to Jeremy, her meeting had run late and she wanted to get things cleaned up at her desk so she could get out. The backpack in the car with what she needed for the weekend with Leo was waiting.

•••

When she got back from Portland on Sunday, Shannon found a note taped to her front door. It was another apology from Jeremy. He promised not to bother her again but asked once more for her to call.

She tore the note in half and dumped it in the recycling.

In only a month, she had gotten closer to Leo than she'd been in almost two years of being with Jeremy. The contrast between the two men couldn't have been starker in ways both big and small. In the past weekend alone, she'd laughed with Leo more than in the whole time she'd been with Jeremy. Leo put her needs and interests on a par with his, often ahead of his. Jeremy never had. Even now, he wanted to get back with her because he had decided it was what he wanted and needed. He'd never mentioned and certainly didn't seem to have considered what she wanted.

Leo accepted who and what she was without question. For heavens sake, he'd sought out something special for her to drink when they had dinner at her house. Jeremy seemed to have forgotten she didn't drink alcohol.

There were a dozen more differences. It was a no brainer. She had no interest in going back to what she'd had—or realized now what she hadn't had—with Jeremy.

Over the next couple of weeks, Jeremy kept his word, sort of. He left a note at the reception desk in city hall a couple times saying he was checking in to see how she was. And he sent a box of what he said were her favorite chocolates on what he said was the anniversary of their first date. It was the wrong day and he had sent his favorite candy, not hers. Leo wanted her to report her ex—who he called "a spineless, sotted shit of a man"—for stalking, but she didn't feel stalked so she didn't. Jeremy wasn't showing up at her work or home unannounced. But Leo insisted the messages and gifts could be interpreted as stalking.

When she said she had a slight twinge of guilt about the way she'd brushed Jeremy off without any consideration of how he might feel, Leo thought she was being much too generous about someone who didn't deserve her.

It was the only thing they disagreed about and even then, not violently.

The pattern they'd begun in April carried them into May—one weekend at her place, the next at his. When they were in Vancouver, they went to First Friday art openings and took Walter to Frenchman's Bar so he could splash in the still chilly waters of the Columbia River. When they were in Portland, they biked on the East Esplanade along the Willamette and went to hear local musicians play. Shannon was sure she'd look back on the spring she met Jeremy as the best one of her life.

Even her job seemed more settled. She'd seen the department's preliminary budget for the year, and in spite of her fears, her job was still there. There were more rounds of negotiations to go but so far, other than the fact she wouldn't be getting a merit raise, it looked all right.

She should have known it was too good to last. The other shoe dropped just after Memorial Day when Marty Morgan showed up on the doorstep of her home.

She was sure the shock she felt was visible on her face. "Daddy. How did you find … what are you … ?" She couldn't seem to finish a sentence. She was too busy trying to decide whether she should throw her arms around him and hug him or slam the door in his face.

"Oh, sweetheart. I could find you anyplace. You're my daughter." He had a huge grin on his face, the one he always had when he dropped back into her life. The one he also had on his face when he walked away. "Aren't you going to ask me in?"

"I was just on my way out," she lied. She hated herself for it, but she was caught so off-guard by his appearance, she wanted some time to collect herself before she talked with him.

His quick once-over, she knew, saw nothing but ratty jeans and an old sweatshirt. "Must not be important. You're certainly not dressed nicely."

"Meeting a girlfriend for coffee and I'm late. Maybe we can get together later this week. Are you here for long?" She knew she sounded uptight, but she didn't want to deal with him right now.

"I'm here for a while. I want to catch up with you. It's been too long. How about dinner on Friday? I have a couple important things to talk to you about."

"Dinner? Okay, I guess. Where? What time?"

"How about the restaurant right down the street from you? Is it any good? Do you like eating there?"

"The Grant House? I like it all right. But I need to eat early. I have plans for the evening." It was her weekend in Portland with Leo, so she'd have to skip dinner with him and arrive late. But she had no intention of missing out on any more of their weekend other than that.

"I'll make the reservation for six-thirty. Early enough for you?" Without waiting for an answer, he leaned in and kissed her cheek. "I can't wait to spend some time with you."

As soon as he walked down the street to the parking area, she made a big show of closing the curtains on the windows and turning on the porch light then leaving in an obvious manner for the tenant's parking lot behind the house. She didn't think her father would follow her to see if she was making up a story, but she drove to a nearby coffee house anyway, went inside, and nursed a latte until she thought it was safe to go back to her house.

Damn. First Jeremy. Now her father. Could her life get any more complicated?

Chapter Eleven

When Shannon arrived at the Grant House on Friday, the host announced, as he crossed out her name on his list, that the other three people were already there.

The other three? Who else had her father brought with him? It appeared things were getting more complicated, whether she liked it or not.

The host led her through the main dining area, where generations of high-ranking officers and their wives once entertained their guests, to the smaller sleeping porch in the back. There was more privacy there, especially when, like tonight, only one party was there—her father, a woman and … and … Jeremy? What the hell?

The two men stood when she approached the table. She kissed her father's cheek. The host pulled out the only empty chair at the table—the one next to her ex-boyfriend. Jeremy tried to take her hand. She pulled away as subtly as she could without making a scene.

Her father was beaming. "I want you to meet someone special, Shannon. This is Louise Hawer. Louise, this is my lovely daughter, Shannon."

"Yes, hello." Shannon regretted the snippy tone of her voice as soon as the words were out. It wasn't fair to the woman looking so expectantly with her hand out in greeting.

Louise had a kind look. She wasn't particularly pretty, although she had nice features. She wasn't the usual rode-hard-and-put-away-wet kind of woman her father had introduced her to before. "Marty's told me so much about you," Louise said, "and how close you are. It's nice to finally meet you. I'm sorry to ambush you like this. I wanted to do this in a more gradual manner, but you know how impulsive your father can be." She tipped up one corner of her mouth in a shy smile and Marty stroked her hand.

How close she was to her father? What fantasy had her father sold this woman? Shannon said, "I'm happy Daddy arranged for us to meet. But I'm puzzled about why Jeremy's included."

"I thought it would be nice," her father said, "for you to have a friend here when I tell you my news."

"Jeremy is my *ex*-boyfriend, Daddy. We broke up over a year ago."

"Jeremy told me all about it. But he's still your friend. And he tells me he wants to pick up where you left off."

"How did you find my father?" she asked Jeremy. "Or how did he find you?"

"We've been in touch off and on for a couple years."

"A couple years?" She turned to her father, not sure whether to be surprised or angry or both. "Is that how you knew where I lived?"

"Jeremy told me he was back in Vancouver and where you … "

The scene was interrupted by the server coming to take drink orders. For the first time in her life, Shannon wished she drank alcohol. She shook her head when asked what she wanted, and the other three ordered a bottle of wine to share.

When the server left, her father said. "Please, don't be upset. I was trying to make this evening easier on you. I have some good news to share and some sad news, too. The good news is Louise and I are getting married and we want you to be part of our wedding."

"Congratulations. If you're happy, I'm happy for you," Shannon said.

"I hoped you'd get to know Louise a bit during this visit. Maybe we could all spend some time together before we go back home."

Perhaps getting to know the woman he was about to marry could help her figure out how to solve the riddle of who her father was. It might be worth a try. Nothing else had worked.

"I have some other important news to tell you." Marty glanced over at Jeremy who nodded before continuing. "Your grandfather passed away last week."

"Granddad died? Was he sick? Why didn't you call me and let me know so I could see him one last time?" Shannon could feel yet another piece of her tattered family fall away with the death of the last relative from whom she had ever felt genuine love.

"It was a sudden heart attack. No one even knew he had heart problems. I decided I'd let you know in person because I knew you'd be upset. Besides, seeing you would give me the opportunity to introduce you to Louise. I knew it would be better for you this way. Balance the sad news with the good."

Why did he do this every time? Dropping back into her life— again—thinking he knew who she was and what she needed when he hadn't been around long enough to know her at all. It was painful and frustrating, and she felt like crying at his insensitive behavior. Again.

"Daddy, you should have let me know sooner. I would have gone to the memorial service at least, even if I couldn't have gotten to see him before he died."

"There wasn't any service. Most of his friends have already passed, so it was pointless to have one when no one would show up. He wanted to be cremated and we did that. We'll do something with his ashes eventually. I'll let you know when we do so you can be there."

"I would have shown up even if no one else was there. This is really upsetting, Daddy."

"That's exactly why I wanted Jeremy here for you."

"He never knew Granddad. Why did you think he'd understand?" Shannon pushed her chair back ready to leave. "I don't think I'm hungry anymore. I think I should go home."

Louise leaned over the table and took her hand. "Shannon, you don't know me from Adam's off-ox so asking a favor might be out of line. I'm sorry Marty put you in this awkward position, but can you try, just for dinner, to put up with it so we can get to know each other a bit? I'd appreciate it if you would."

Louise sounded sincere. Shannon didn't want to hurt her. And she didn't want to screw up her father's chances of finally having someone normal to be with. Although, God knows, he had never worried about her feelings in the same way, as his handling of the news of her grandfather's death proved.

Finally, she sighed. "All right. Just for dinner." She picked up her menu and pretended to read it.

She was distracted by the host seating another couple at a nearby table. They looked like a young couple in love, holding hands, sitting next to each other, smiling, looking at each other like lovers do. Like Leo looked at her. If only it was Leo here with her instead of Jeremy. Maybe she could call him and he could come join them. No, as tempting as it was to run to the ladies' room and text him to come rescue her, with the traffic, by the time he got to Vancouver from Portland, dinner would be over. She'd have to wait to see him until he came to pick her up at seven-thirty.

The conversation after they ordered their meals was awkward, and for Shannon, pointless. At the same time she was trying to process the death of her grandfather and her father's off-handed dismissal of her disappointment about not seeing him again, she felt compelled to make small talk with Louise. She ended up liking her. The poor woman didn't understand the drama going on at the table, and she didn't deserve the situation Marty Morgan had put her in.

While Shannon was making a stab at conversation with Louise, Jeremy was talking softly with her father. She could only make out a few words. Most of it seemed to be about his hike from Canada to Mexico on the Pacific Crest Trail. From what little she heard, every step had been over hot coals and every night had been spent fighting off hungry wolves and Bigfoot. But some of it, in whispers, really, was about something else—something about money. Maybe Jeremy was borrowing money from her father until he got a job. Maybe vice versa. She couldn't hear the details and didn't care anyway. It wasn't anything to do with her.

The conversation didn't get any less stilted between the four of them when their main courses arrived. Everyone ate quickly, and as soon as the plates were cleared, Shannon pushed her chair back. "I'm sorry to eat and run, but I have plans for this evening."

"Wait. There's something more I have to tell you, Shannon," her father said.

"Then tell me quickly. I have a date waiting for me," she said.

"Your grandfather left a will. There are certain provisions you don't need to know about, but one might interest you. He left you some family heirlooms—several pieces of your grandmother's jewelry and a little money."

Her throat closed in a lump she had to swallow hard to talk around. "Gramma's pearls?"

"Yes, and her engagement ring. I have them with me in my hotel room. We'll have to get together again so I can give them to you. And we haven't talked about the wedding yet." He turned to Louise and patted her hand. "We'll do that, too, the next time."

Leave it to her father to use her inheritance as leverage to get what he wanted. Now she wondered if the sadness she'd been feeling all evening was only because of the news about her grandfather. Maybe some of it was because her father was doing what he always did—frustrating and disappointing her.

"Okay. Call me later." She glanced at her phone. "I really need to go. I'm late now."

"I'll walk you home," Jeremy said, putting his napkin on the table and beginning to stand.

"Jeremy, I live right down the street. I don't need anyone to walk me home. Besides, my date will be waiting."

"Don't be rude, Shannon," her father said. "Jeremy's only being a gentleman."

"I doubt that, Daddy." She dug in her purse and pulled out her wallet. "How much do I owe you for dinner?" She was anxious to get out of the restaurant before she made a fool of herself either by crying or by saying something she'd later regret.

"Now you're insulting me. I invited you. You're my guest."

"Thank you, then." She pushed back her chair, wanting to bolt for the door but remembered in time to say something to the puzzled looking woman sitting across from her. "Nice to meet you, Louise."

Before his fiancée could respond, Marty said, "When will I see you again, sweetheart?"

"I don't know. I'm awfully busy at work. I'll be in touch."

As she race-walked out of the sleeping porch, she heard him say, "Wait, you don't have my cell phone number!"

Blowing past the host and several people waiting to be seated, Shannon was close to a run by the time she got to the sidewalk, so eager was she to get away from the awkward dinner scene. When she saw Leo waiting for her on her front porch, she was glad she'd hurried.

She ran up the steps and threw her arms around him. "I'm so glad to see you," she said. "I am a walking disaster with a soap opera life, and you should probably run away before I drag you any deeper into it."

He put his arm around her shoulder and kissed the tip of her nose. "You're not a disaster and the soap opera comment intrigues me. Since I'm not going anywhere except where you want to go, you'll have a chance to tell me about it. Sounds like you need someone to have your back right now. Let me."

"You're such a good friend."

He pulled away from her embrace. "Is that what we are? Friends?"

She couldn't see his face in the shadow, didn't know where to take the conversation. "Well, we are friends. And we're lovers, too. Is that what you mean?"

"What I mean, Shannon, is I think of us as more than friends and fuck buddies. Do you?"

She wasn't sure whether to laugh or cry. Now even Leo, who she'd thought would be her refuge, was pushing her emotional buttons. "Fuck buddies?"

"Okay, lovers. Whatever. You didn't answer the question. Do you want to be more than friends and lovers?"

She stood on tiptoes and kissed him gently, hoping she could divert his attention from her lack of response. On the heels of an awkward dinner with her father and her ex-boyfriend, who'd spent as much time talking to each other as they had to the women with them, the last thing she needed was another man asking her for something. She'd gone from no men in her personal life to three in record time and she didn't know how to deal with it. And hadn't she told Powell that her relationship with Leo was just about sex? It was, wasn't it?

If it wasn't, she didn't know what to do about it.

Leo must have picked up on her mood. "My timing sucks, doesn't it? Sounds like you've already had a rough evening and here I am trying to push you into a place you're not comfortable being. I'm sorry. I don't want to make things any more difficult. I just want you to know how special I think you are."

Shannon smiled up at him, relieved. Trying to lighten up the conversation, she said, "If I'm not sure yet what I want does that mean we can't be fuck buddies?"

"Hell, yes, we can. I'm not stupid." Taking her cue, he said, "I spend all week thinking about how many times and how many ways I'm gonna make love to you when the weekend rolls around. In fact, you're getting to be a menace. One of these days, I'm gonna burn the hell out of me or Giles because I'm so distracted thinking about you."

"Good. I mean I don't want you injured but I'd like to think I could distract you as much as you distract me. Powell says … "

"When do I get to meet this woman, by the way?" he interrupted.

"Next weekend at my house. I thought I'd invite her and her latest … well, in her case he probably *is* a fuck buddy … for dinner. She's dying to meet you, too." She moved out of the shadow toward the door. "Oh, but if she calls you Studly-Do-Right, don't ask any questions, okay?"

Leo followed her into the house, a huge smile on his face. "I won't ask any questions, but I sure as hell would like to know why she calls me that."

"I'll never tell. Although she may." Shannon glanced around her living room, the temporary respite from her confused thoughts over. She wasn't sure what she was looking for but suspected it wasn't something she was likely to find there anyway. Because, really, would a couple pieces of furniture give her the answer about how to deal with the men who were responsible for making her life so complicated?

But Leo interpreted her look differently. "It looks like you might want to stay here tonight, in your own place."

"God, no. I can hardly wait to get away from here. And if we stayed here, what would Walter do all alone?"

"Walter I can take care of. I want to make sure you're taken care of first." He dropped a kiss on the top of her head.

Chapter Twelve

Leo rented a small, one story house in southeast Portland close enough to his studio so he could bicycle there. The house reminded Shannon of a hobbit cottage with its A-frame shingled roof and old, well-established shrubs and bushes. Inside, the tiny kitchen, two bedrooms, one bath, combination living room and dining room felt warm and cozy. Leo wasn't exactly an interior decorator, but he had an instinct for design and a love for color she assumed came from being an artist. The furnishings were minimal—bookshelves, a couch and side chair, coffee table, dining room table and four chairs—but the style was clean and the colors he used, striking. The couch was upholstered in a dark blue fabric; the pillows thrown on it were shades of green, except for one yellow one. The side chair was pale yellow. The rug was an abstract design of blues, yellows, and a bit of green.

And there was glass everywhere—a bowl on the coffee table, light sconces on the wall in the dining area, vessels of various sizes and shapes in the book shelves. The first time she'd been there, Shannon had spent so much time looking at all his glass, Leo had had to kiss her hard to get her attention back on him.

As soon as they arrived and greeted Walter, Leo said, "Sit for a minute and tell me what happened."

After she gave him the highlights of the dreadful dinner with her father, his fiancée and her ex, he said, "I know something that may make you feel better. Why don't you feed Walter and let me get it ready for you?"

"Thanks but you don't really have to. I don't think I have enough room for any more food tonight."

"It's not food. It's a surprise."

"Okay, I'll bite. What kind of surprise?"

He looked at her with amusement. "Unclear on the concept of surprise, are you? Be patient. Relax for a bit and I'll show you."

She went into the pantry, put kibble into Walter's bowl, and changed his water. Whatever Leo was doing entailed opening and closing lots of drawers in the living and dining rooms and a bit of cursing under his breath. He disappeared down the hall before she got Walter settled. The dog gobbled down his food then joined her in the living room where he attempted to jump up beside her on the couch, a no-no but he always tried anyway, as if to see if she remembered.

About fifteen minutes later, Leo returned, barefoot with his shirtsleeves rolled up and a necktie in his hand. "Ready?"

"Sure. Where're we going?"

"I'm going to put this over your eyes so you can't see and … "

"Is the surprise some kinky sex thing?"

"Damn. I never thought about a kinky sex thing. I'll have to remember that for another time. You'll have to settle for what I put together tonight." He motioned for her to stand. "Close your eyes." He tied the tie around her head so her eyes were mostly covered. "Too tight? Or uncomfortable?"

"No, it's fine. Now what?"

"Now I'm going to take you to the surprise." From behind, he gently guided her in the direction he wanted her to go. When he stopped, she smelled something flowery, sweet. And she could hear soft instrumental music, the kind played in spas or as background for meditation.

He slipped the tie down around her neck and said, "Voila."

While he undid the knot and removed the tie, she blinked so she could focus. He'd led her to the bathroom, not the bedroom. The overhead light was off. In the huge claw foot tub she'd never used, opting for the stall shower, he had drawn a bath and filled it with bubbles. Around the room, on the shelf above the sink and the windowsill, on the radiator and the back of the toilet, were candles—maybe a dozen of them—each one in a glass vessel, cup or vase of some sort so the light from the candles glowed through the glass in jewel-like colors. Looking more closely at several vessels, Shannon could see the candles didn't quite match the elegance of the candleholders but it hardly mattered.

"Oh, Leo, it's beautiful. Did you make all those candleholders?"

"Yeah, experimental stuff, some from years ago. Sorry I couldn't find nice candles, they're mostly the ones I have in case of a power failure but … "

"It doesn't matter. The light through your glass is gorgeous."

"Thanks." He looked almost embarrassed by her praise. "I thought you should soak for a while, relax, let some of the last few hours go. Then I'll wash your hair and give you a massage."

She began to tear up. "No one's ever done anything like this for me before."

"Hey, no tears. This was supposed to make you happy. You deserve pampering after the soap opera evening you had." He pulled at the bottom of her shirt to get it out from the waistband of her skirt. "Let's get you undressed and into the water before it cools off any more."

She noticed he was taking his time with the buttons on her shirt. The object seemed to be getting the shirt unfastened without touching her. "You're being awfully careful with the unbuttoning," Shannon said.

"If I'm not careful, this lovely spa scene will go completely to waste because I will have hauled you off to bed."

She laughed. "Will we end up there for my massage?"

"That's the plan." He had her shirt off and was working on the front hook of her bra. "I didn't really think this through about undressing you, did I? Maybe you better finish it up yourself." He dropped the bra.

As her eyes followed her bra to the ground, she could see a bulge in the front of his jeans, the reason he wanted her to take over. She leaned into him and kissed him gently. "I'll take it from here. But I'll need a hand to get into the tub."

Leo groaned. "Helping a beautiful naked woman into the tub. You're killing me, baby."

When she'd shimmied out of her skirt, panties, and shoes, he took her hand to steady her as she climbed in. After she was settled in the warm water under the cover of bubbles, he handed her a rolled towel to use as a headrest and left, saying he'd be back in fifteen or twenty minutes.

It was heavenly. Muted light. Soft music. Warm water. Sweet smells. Shannon closed her eyes and relaxed for the first time all evening, allowing herself to think only about where she was and who had thought to give her this treat.

She must have dozed off because it seemed like only a few minutes had gone by when Leo came back with a stack of towels and what looked like a bottle of shampoo. The water had cooled a bit, so he warmed it up for her then sluiced it through her hair before working the shampoo in, massaging her scalp and neck before rinsing the soap out.

After helping her out of the tub and into a terrycloth robe, he towel-dried her hair.

Hand in hand, they went the few feet into his bedroom where he slipped off the robe and motioned her to his bed. She lay down on her stomach and he positioned her so there was room at the head of the bed for him to kneel. As soon as she was settled she heard him squirt something onto his hands, smelled a clean herbal scent, then felt him begin to smooth lotion over her heat-softened muscles.

Starting with her shoulders and upper arms, Leo rubbed and kneaded, using his thumbs in some places, his whole hand in others, completing what the hot water had begun to relax her. He knew exactly what to do and how to do it. Shannon was sure she moaned almost constantly, it felt so good.

Working his way down her back, a vertebra at a time, he reached her bottom, which he treated with the same care and attention. By the time he returned to her shoulders and neck, she was not only completely relaxed but also wanting more from him than merely a rubdown.

"It's time to turn over, isn't it?" She matched her actions to her words. "I usually have a sheet to cover me when I get a massage. Do I need one?" She tried to look like she was asking an innocent question when she met his gaze, but she was sure it wasn't working.

"No, not with me. With anyone else, hell yes, you need a sheet." His voice was thick, raspy. He cleared his throat once or twice, but the flash of desire across his face and his inability to take his eyes off her breasts said he was probably not going to get the neediness out of his voice with a simple cough.

He leaned over her and touched his mouth to hers. She thought it was funny at first, kissing upside down. But it didn't take long before she stopped thinking and only felt.

His mouth—nibbling at her lower lip then capturing her whole mouth with his. His hands—moving slowly, very, very slowly, massaging again. She arched her back, encouraging him to touch her breasts, to move further down and touch her sex. But he was not in a hurry it seemed. He broke from the kiss and sat up to continue his massage. She groaned in frustration but he only smiled as he moved north again, to her temples, her eyebrows, and her cheeks, tracing the bones in her face with a soft touch and gentle pressure. Then he went to her neck and shoulders and began a slow, thorough path to her ribs, her waist, and her belly.

Bypassing her breasts, he allowed his fingers to stray into the triangle of damp curls at the top of her thighs. She raised her hips and he began to touch her where she wanted him, in the hot core of her, giving her clitoris the same careful attention he'd given all the rest of her body.

She was edgy with need now. She reached over her head and yanked at his shirt, trying to pull it from the waistband of his jeans.

When he startled at the suddenness of her move, she said, "It's time for you to be part of this, too." She dropped the shirttail and grabbed his hands. "I want you beside me. Now."

"Whatever the lady wants tonight, the lady gets." He moved from the head of the bed and knelt astride her. "Upside down, right side up, up to your neck in bubbles, or naked in my bed, you're the most beautiful thing I've ever seen in all my life. I don't know how I lucked out, having you here." Leo finished the job of removing his shirt, but before he could get to his jeans, she unsnapped and unzipped him, releasing his cock from his boxers and pulling him down beside her. When she had him where she wanted him, she dragged off his jeans and underwear. Once he was as naked as she was, she took his penis in her hand and began a slow, steady massage of her own. She didn't break eye contact, wanting to see desire in his eyes, hear his breathing become as ragged as her own. And when she heard it, she dipped her head and took him in her mouth.

His erection was velvet-covered steel, and tasted of sea and salt. She could hear in his uneven breathing and occasional moan the effect she had on him. But what she had intended to arouse him further was doing the same for her. Cupping his balls and swirling her tongue over the head of his penis, she felt her body soften and catch fire as they both moved closer to the inevitable.

•••

Jesus, this woman was going to kill him. First undressing her in the bathroom and now this. He wasn't sure how much longer he could keep himself from spilling into her mouth. But he didn't know how—didn't know if he really wanted—to stop her from what she was doing. She was making little noises at the back of her throat, the kind she made when she was about to come, only now the sound vibrated on his cock like nothing he'd ever felt before.

It took all his will power to pull away from her. "We need to get a condom on me. Right now." He rolled to his side and grabbed a foil packet from the nightstand. She ripped it open and covered him then rose to her knees, straddling him, and slowly, inch-by-inch lowered herself. When he was fully enclosed by her, she leaned over, her hands on either side of his head, her damp hair tickling his chest.

"Show me how you want it, baby," Leo whispered.

She began slowly, establishing a rocking rhythm, gradually picking up speed until he knew he wasn't going to last much longer. Holding her hip with one hand, he found her clitoris again with the other and massaged one last time to bring her to orgasm. As her inner muscles closed around him, he came too, calling her name.

Shannon collapsed on him, seeming to have no ability to remain upright. When she shivered as the sweat from their exertions cooled, he pulled the sheet and blanket up over her and held her close until they were breathing normally.

"I see fireworks when we make love," she said. "You make me see fireworks."

He wiped away a tear leaking from her eye. "We make them together, baby."

However, relaxing in afterglow apparently wasn't part of the plan. At least, it wasn't Walter's plan. The dog had managed to nose open the door, which Leo, in his haste to get Shannon into his bed, hadn't quite shut all the way. Walter trotted into the bedroom and went from one side of the bed to the other trying to get someone to pay attention to him. Shannon volunteered to take him out but Leo insisted she stay in bed while he took care of the dog and made sure he'd gotten all the candles out.

By the time he got back, she was sound asleep.

Chapter Thirteen

Shannon woke with the first light and, cocooned in the comforter on Leo's bed, replayed the events of the night before. She couldn't believe it was possible to go from sadness and frustration to feeling happier than she could remember being in a long time. But she had. All because of Leo. It wasn't only that she loved the way he touched her and made love to her, although he was amazing. It wasn't just that he could be counted on, no questions asked. It was more about how sweet he was, how concerned he was about how she felt.

When she was a little girl, she'd dreamed of having her father rescue her from life with an alcoholic mother. He'd never come through. When she was older, she'd hoped to find a man who would love her as much as she loved him. She'd never found him.

But here was a man who did the most thoughtful things for her, made her feel beautiful and desirable, who had her back, as he described it, and wanted her to know how special she was. No one had ever done all that for her before. Could she have finally found what she'd wanted all these years? The thought both excited and frightened her. What if she was wrong? What if Leo wasn't the knight on the white horse she thought he was? What if he was like the others? Could she take one more disappointment?

Before she could come to any conclusion or answer any of her own questions, an arm came around her waist and a now awake—and obviously aroused—Leo began to nibble on her neck. "Good morning," she said as she rolled over and pecked his cheek.

"Any morning when I wake up with you in my bed is a good morning," he said. "But do you really think what you did qualifies as a wake-up kiss? I don't. Let me show you what does."

While he thoroughly kissed her, he insinuated one leg between hers and wrapped his arms around her. Drawing back slightly from her mouth, he whispered. "And now I'll show you what makes a good morning perfect."

• • •

"How about I make you my world-famous French toast for breakfast?" Leo asked. He'd made coffee and was enjoying the sight of her petting Walter. He wasn't sure which was more fun to watch—Walter leaning into her hand or Shannon making sure she petted all the places she knew the dog liked.

"World famous, huh?" she said, looking up from her task with a smile.

"Okay, it's only well known among a small group of family and friends. But my family and friends have always been my world. Now, you get to join this select group."

"I'd love to. It sounds delicious."

The kitchen was quiet as the three of them—Shannon, Leo, and Walter—enjoyed the sights and smells of a lazy Saturday morning. Walter was being petted. Shannon was being spoiled. Leo was being … well, he was being smug about how good his life had been since Shannon had been in it. So smug he almost burned the French toast.

Luckily, he didn't. And Shannon joined the group who loved his cooking. In fact, she complimented him on his cooking skills so many times, he finally said, "You don't have to thank me for breakfast, it's my pleasure to have you here. And I do mean pleasure."

She flushed red for a moment and played with her fork before saying, "Okay, if I can't thank you for breakfast, how about I thank you for last night. Or would it be too weird? What you did when we came home—came here—was beyond anything I could have even imagined. I owe you."

"You don't owe me anything. It's what someone does for the person they care for." He watched her face carefully to see what her reaction would be.

She looked down at the table for a moment and fiddled with her fork again before asking, "Care for?"

"Yeah. Make you nervous?"

"A little." She finally looked up and half smiled.

He grinned at her. "Deal with it." He was relieved she hadn't run screaming from the house at his declaration.

"I think I can. But I still owe you."

"That's not how I operate, but if you insist, how about paying me back by letting me ask you something about your father."

She was biting her lip, the little frown back between her eyes. "I'm not sure I can tell you much about him. Even though I have his last name, I can't say I know him well. What do you want to know?"

In spite of her nervousness, he plowed ahead, wanting to solve the mystery of why she so desperately needed the man's attention. "Let's start with the easy stuff. What's he do for a living?"

"He sells things."

"Things?"

"He's sold insurance and cars, real estate, and cell phone service. I'm not sure what he's selling now. He's made a lot of money over the years because he's good at selling. But he's not so good at knowing what to do with the money he earns. He's lost almost as much as he's made investing in businesses that didn't work out. According to my mother—who, you have to understand, isn't the world's most unbiased source on this subject—he's always convinced he'll hit the jackpot in the next deal. Like he's always convinced the next woman will be the right one."

"How long were your parents married?"

"I don't know for sure if they were. There are no wedding photos anywhere in the family albums. And my mom just says they were together for six years. My dad brushed it off the one time I tried to ask him. He left us … "

"Left your mother," Leo said firmly.

Shannon shook her head. "Okay, if you insist. He left *my mother* when I was five. I didn't see him again until I was ten. My mom hated it when he wanted to see me, tried to keep him away from me. When I could drive, it got easier. He'd call once or twice a year, and I'd go meet him for lunch. About the time I graduated from high school, he moved to Reno. Since then he's dropped in sometimes, long enough to make me hope he wants a real relationship but not long enough to make it happen."

She picked up her coffee cup and drained the rest of the brew from it, got up, refilled her cup, then continued. "My grandparents, his mom and dad, kept in touch with me so I knew where he was, what he was doing. I was their only grandchild, so they made sure I saw and heard from them. A couple years ago, Gramma died and Granddad ended up in assisted living because he couldn't take care of himself. When Daddy told me last night that Granddad died, it really upset me. The last time I saw him was about eight months ago when I was visiting my mother. I wish I'd had the chance to see him one more time."

"How come your father didn't tell you your grandfather was sick?"

"He says it's because his death was sudden. But I think it's more likely he just didn't think to call me. Now he's here with some story about a will and needing to get some jewelry and a bit of money to me. Then there's the new girlfriend I told you about last night, the one he says he's marrying soon. I can't keep up with his stories. I sometimes wonder why I even try."

"It must be hard to get your hopes up and have him let you down."

"It is. And yet I keep hoping. Keep feeling like a loser when the same thing happens again."

"You're not a loser. He is. He's lost out on being part of his incredible daughter's life. You haven't needed him to become an awesome adult. You've done fine without him."

"Thank you. But still ... I don't know ... I want him to acknowledge I matter to him, to think of me as his daughter instead of somebody he sees every few years, like an old high school classmate you only see at the occasional reunion. He knows less about me than he does his customers, I bet. And still I keep beating my head against this wall around him trying to get him to let me in."

"I can't imagine how frustrating it must be for you."

She looked at him with shiny eyes. "It is. And this time, it's not only frustrating but it's weirder than usual. He suddenly has Jeremy as his new best friend. That I really don't understand. Daddy said he invited Jeremy last night so I'd have a friend with me when I got the bad news about Granddad."

"How did he even know where to find Jeremy?"

"My question exactly. Apparently they hit it off when they met while Jeremy and I were dating. I guess they've been in touch with each other since then. But Daddy must know we haven't seen each other in over a year. Surely Jeremy hasn't been that dishonest with him."

Leo reached across the table for her hand. "Hmm. Maybe your life does have certain elements in common with *All My Children*. Although there's been no murder or hidden twin." He gave her a fake surprised look. "Or are you saving that to tell me later?"

"No, no one died mysteriously and I'm quite sure I was a single birth." She squeezed his hand. "You can make me laugh even when I'm feeling crummy. I like that about you."

"Thank you, ma'am. I aim to please. If I can't convince you to like me with my artistic talents and my cooking, I'll take convincing you with my attempts at humor."

"The other two work. So does the way you … well …I guess it's the way you, you know, take care of me."

"You've been responsible for yourself for a long time now, haven't you?"

"Yeah, between my father's inattention and my mother's love for the bottle, I've been on my own for most of my life."

"No wonder you don't know how to react when someone cares for you, takes care of you."

The more Shannon talked the more it became clear why she was so reluctant to say how she felt about him. What would it take to convince her he was serious about wanting to be more than a friend? Would she always hold back something to protect herself? He was as determined to do what it took to breach those walls as she was to do what it took to get her father's attention. Maybe even more so. He just wasn't sure how to do it.

"It's always been something I've done myself. For myself."

"Doesn't have to be, you know. I … " His phone buzzed and he glanced at the screen. It was a text from Giles Kaye, saying there was an emergency at the studio. "Shit. Hold the thought. I have to see what this is about."

Leo called the studio. Giles was frantic. One of the annealing ovens was down; Giles was on deadline for a project; the guy who was supposed to be helping him was AWOL; a piece of his project had thermo-shocked and had to be recreated.

Leo stopped him before Giles could list any more disasters. "I'll be right there. But I have company. All right if she watches?"

"As long as she stays out of the way and lets you alone long enough to get me out of this mess, you can bring the entire Thorns soccer team as far as I'm concerned."

"We're at my house and about to finish breakfast. We'll be there soon."

•••

Although Shannon had never been in any kind of artist's studio, much less a glass studio, she thought she knew what one would look like. The GlassCo studio didn't fit the image. Leo led her through a large, metal, garage-type roll up door into an industrial looking building. There was nothing artsy about it.

On one side of a large open space two furnaces holding a yellow-orange substance gave off a great deal of heat. Opposite the furnaces was a wall of metal boxes of various sizes, a few with doors open so she could see what looked like bricks lining the inside. In the back were two long tables, and behind them, she saw shelves crowded with jars of colored granules and long tubes of colored spaghetti-looking sticks. A woman was working there wearing safety glasses and maneuvering large sheets of glass. A man was pacing in front of the tables.

As soon as the man noticed their arrival, he stopped pacing. "Leo, thank God you're here. I can't believe the mess I'm in."

"We'll get it squared away." Leo took his arm from around Shannon's shoulders and waved in the general direction of the two people. "Shannon, meet Giles Kaye and Amanda St. Claire. Everybody, this is Shannon Morgan."

Amanda smiled and said, "It's nice to meet the woman who's put such a big grin on Leo's face lately." She removed her glasses, walked out from behind the table, and held out her hand.

"Nice to meet you, too," Shannon said. "I've seen pictures of your work in the paper. It's so uncomplicated and yet so complex. It really draws you in. I loved it."

"And I love the way you describe it. Thanks."

"Okay, enough small talk," Giles said. "Sorry to ruin your day by making you hang out here watching us work, Shannon, but I'm desperate."

"I'm happy to have a chance to watch you blow glass. The only time I've ever seen anyone work with glass was at the Clark County Fair. There's a guy there who makes little glass animals."

"Oh, Dave. Yeah, he's good," Giles said. "I like his work, too."

While the two men got things ready to work on Giles's project, Amanda gave Shannon a quick tour of the studio. She pointed out the glory holes full of molten glass and the equipment the glass blowers used, then she showed off the sheet glass, stringer, and frit—what Shannon thought looked like spaghetti and granules— she used for her kiln-formed glass. Lastly, she indicated what they all shared—a wall of kilns and annealing ovens and the small office at the back.

Something Amanda didn't explain caught Shannon's eye in the office. "What's all that?" she asked, pointing to long, thin and carefully separated tubes of blown glass stacked on what appeared to be temporary shelving along one wall of the office.

"Ah, you've discovered one of our problems these days," Amanda said. "Those are the pieces for Leo's fireworks. He keeps making more of them, and we're running out of storage space. For a while he was taking them home but Walter got into them. Broke some and damaged others so they're here until he can find a safe place to store them."

"I may have a solution to your problem," Shannon said as she inspected the pieces. Before she could explain what her solution was she saw five pieces, blocks of glass with subtle designs in spectacular colors. "This is your work, isn't it? It's wonderful. The colors are beautiful! I had no idea glass came in all these shades."

"It is mine and thanks. The colors are one of the reasons most of us do what we do. Just when we think we've used all the colors possible in our work, Bullseye brings out new ones and we're addicted again." To the puzzled look on Shannon's face, Amanda responded, "Bullseye manufactures the glass we use. Their factory and retail store are not too far from here. Have Leo take you there some day. It's like a candy store for glass artists, but it's even pretty to look at if you don't work with the material."

Amanda picked up two folding chairs propped against a set of cabinets and handed one to Shannon. "The guys should be ready to work by now. Let's go sit out of their way and watch them. It's fascinating. I still love to watch, even after we've lived in each other's laps for all these years."

"I don't mean to drag you away from your work," Shannon said as they left the office.

"You're not. I was finishing up when you got here. All my pieces are in the kilns cooking." She indicated the metal boxes.

"What's the project Giles is working on?" Shannon asked as they watched the two men select long rods from an assortment on a pair of sawhorses.

"It's called 'The Flowering of Peace.' It's for a peace-themed exhibit in San Francisco. He's designed three round, petal-shaped bowls, one inside the other, the small center one holding even smaller glass balls to represent the seeds of peace. I think there's a dove involved somehow, too, but I'm not sure. It's pretty complicated. To get the pieces to adhere, the layers all have to be the same temperature or they won't fuse. And if the pieces are unevenly heated, one piece might crack."

"Like when you put ice into a glass fresh from the dishwasher drying cycle?"

"Exactly. Glass doesn't like to change temperatures too fast. That's what happened to Giles's piece. He had the outer layer and the small open round at temp but apparently not the second layer. It cracked when he was putting what he thought was the almost finished piece into the annealing oven for a cool-down. So now he has to redo the whole thing. It set him back in what was already a tight schedule."

As Shannon watched, the two men donned glasses with smoked lenses to protect their eyes against the intense light of the molten glass and then began to recreate the first of the broken pieces. Amanda explained how Leo was using a blowpipe to collect a gather of glass from the glory hole, the furnace full of molten glass, then with a puff or two, blowing a bubble of glass which Giles molded into the shape he wanted, his hands protected by thick pads of newspaper. When it was the size Giles wanted it to be, he attached a punty, one of the long rods on the sawhorses, to the bottom of the piece and the bubble was released from the blowpipe. After it went back into the fire to reheat it, a hole was cut in the top to form the bowl shape and Giles could work to create the petals. Not happy with the first one, Giles got rid of the piece and the process started all over again.

It took three tries for Giles to be satisfied with the shape of the bowl. When it was finally right, he applied molten glass in a contrasting color to the edge in what Amanda called a lip wrap.

"I've never seen anything so fascinating," Shannon said.

Amanda smiled. "Fire, hot glass, cute guys playing with it. What about *that* isn't fascinating?"

"They obviously have done this a lot because they're so coordinated in what they do, so graceful. It's like watching a couple of ballet dancers."

Leo groaned. "I think every woman I've ever known who's watched glass blowers at work said that! It's almost like it's … "

Another woman's voice interrupted. "Do you have a lot of women watch you dance, Leo?"

Fortunately, Leo was holding a punty, not a piece of glass, so when he dropped it nothing broke. "Cathy, what're you doing here?" he asked. "Sorry. Didn't mean to be rude. Let me try again. Hello, Cathy, nice to see you."

The woman walked up to him and kissed him on the cheek. Who the hell was this woman that she could just kiss Leo? And not only was he not surprised that she did, but he didn't object. Shannon wasn't sure why it bothered her so much. She didn't own Leo. But when the man with whom you just spent a torrid night as well as a morning of gut-wrenching talk was kissed by a beautiful woman, it made her uncomfortable. Okay, more than uncomfortable. She'd never been jealous of another woman before, but she was pretty sure this was what it felt like.

"You could never be rude, Leo," the woman said. "And to answer your first question, I was over at Bullseye buying glass, and I thought I'd come by to see how you're doing. I haven't seen you in ages. Was the piece you put in to be annealed yours? It looked interesting."

"No, it's Giles's work."

"Now I'm the rude one. Hello, Giles, nice to see you again.

Giles nodded acknowledgement before continuing to clean up the tools they'd been using.

"And, Amanda, it's been a long time since I've seen you, too." Cathy looked at Shannon with an expectant expression on her face. "I'm Cathy Anderson."

"I'm Shannon Morgan."

"Are you a glass artist, too?"

"No, I'm a … "

"She's with me, Cathy," Leo interjected.

"Ah, I see. Well, this is a bit awkward isn't it?" Her laugh sounded brittle as she looked at Leo. "Your past and your present colliding." Turning back to Shannon, she said, "I'm Leo's ex."

Of course she was. Leo had never mentioned her name when they'd swapped breakup stories, but given the way her life had been going lately, it was only to be expected that his ex-girlfriend would not only be another glass artist but also a stunning redhead with a killer body, curved in the right places, voluptuous where it counted, and with the long legs of a dancer. Shannon looked at the other woman's tights and silky tunic then down at her jeans and T-shirt. There was no comparison. Cathy won on all counts.

Amanda stood. "I doubt it's awkward for any of us, Cathy. We're all grown-ups. Want a cup of coffee? We have a Keurig now and have a steady supply of whatever you want to drink."

"Coffee would be great. By the way, I saw your latest work at The Fairchild. It's fascinating. You're still finding interesting things to do with metals and foils, aren't you?"

The two women went into the office in the back, continuing the conversation about their work. Leo took the chair Amanda had vacated and reached for Shannon's hand. "She's never dropped in without warning before. I'm sorry."

"She's gorgeous." The words were out of Shannon's mouth before she could stop them.

Leo frowned a bit. "I guess."

"And she does glass like Amanda does?"

"No, she casts glass. Like Lillian Pitt's mask on the Land Bridge."

Shannon took a deep breath and let it out with a whoosh. "The two of you seem so … I don't know … so civilized, I guess. Neither one acts angry or anything."

"Because we're not. It just didn't work out between us. We both knew it wasn't going well. She was the one who made the break but it was bound to happen."

Giles, who'd been eavesdropping but trying to look like he wasn't, came over and stood in front of the couple. "Amanda and I were rooting for them to end it weeks before they finally did. Leo wasn't pleasant to be around for the last few months they were together. She's a bit of a diva—her work is wonderful and she shows in all the right galleries but the attention has gone to her head. He's much happier with you, believe me."

"Thanks, Giles, I appreciate it," Shannon said. She noticed the grateful look Leo gave Giles.

"And here comes the queen herself," Giles said in a whisper, as Amanda and Cathy came out of the office, both of them carrying mugs.

"Leo, Amanda told me about your wonderful commission in Vancouver," Cathy said. "Congratulations. It sounds exciting. When can I see it?"

"It's a short term installation. It'll go up a few days before the Fourth of July and come down right after."

"Ah, performance art."

"In a manner of speaking, I guess."

"You and Matthew Barney," she said, mentioning the artist known for his elaborate, often brief and quirky, art installations.

"I'm not sitting on a block of ice wearing only Vaseline, no."

"I was speaking metaphorically, Leo." She finished what was in her mug. "Well, I better get my glass home. I have another show opening in three months, and I have only half my work finished for it."

Amanda took the mug. "Nice to see you again, Cathy. Good luck with your show."

"Thanks, Amanda. Back at you." She pecked Leo on the cheek again. "Good luck with the project, Leo." She waved at Giles. "Hope your piece works out, too." She was two steps away from the door when she said, "Oh, and nice to meet you, Sharon."

"Bitch," Giles muttered.

Chapter Fourteen

"You're quiet," Leo said, glancing over at Shannon. She'd been looking out the window on the passenger side of his truck without saying a word since they left the studio, and he hadn't a clue what she was thinking.

She seemed to take a minute to pull her thoughts away from wherever they'd been. "Sorry. I'm thinking about stuff."

"Such as?"

"Well, for one thing, you need a place to store your pieces of glass for the fireworks."

"How do you … ? Oh, right, Amanda must have told you. Yeah, it's getting to be a problem. I can't take the pieces home because of Walter. And all the temporary storage places where I could rent space would require putting in shelving which would be too expensive."

"My second bedroom has bookshelves built along one wall. Would it work to store your glass there?"

"Are you kidding me? Close to the installation site, complete with shelving, and free? That's as perfect as it gets." He looked over at her again. "Oh, uh … maybe I'm assuming too much. Do we need to be talking rental terms?"

She shook her head and a small smile appeared. "Of course not. I wouldn't offer the space if I didn't mean it to be free."

"Then I accept. Thank you. Amanda will be thrilled to get my glass out of the office."

"Why don't we go back and get the pieces now?"

"How about tomorrow? Before I take you home."

"If that's what you want, great." The glass storage settled, Shannon retreated again into silence.

"But where to keep my glass is not what's really bothering you." It wasn't a question.

His prodding was met with another silence for what seemed like a long time. Finally, in a small voice he'd never heard her use, she said, "She's so beautiful."

"Who is? Amanda?" He couldn't figure out what his studio mate had to do with anything.

"Cathy. She's gorgeous and talented and has great clothes and probably kisses like a porn star and … "

"You're jealous?" He stared at her until the light they were waiting at turned green. "You are, aren't you?" He couldn't help it. He grinned.

"No, absolutely not." She shook her head. "Well, maybe a little. A tiny bit." The headshake turned into a nod. "Okay, I'm jealous. She's perfect. And I am decidedly not."

"Let's see, you're jealous of my ex-girlfriend; you tell me your family secrets after a bad evening; you wear sexy underwear for me and you woo my dog with custom-made dog biscuits. Why, Ms. Morgan, I do believe you're beginning to have feelings for me."

"I never said I didn't."

"You sure as hell haven't exactly been open about it." Leo wanted to say more, wanted to call her on her inability to tell him how she felt about their relationship but he was afraid to push too hard and make her run.

"Okay, maybe I haven't been. I've never told a man I … " She stared up at the roof of the truck as if she were hoping to see the space station appear there. "I cared for him."

"Then never said 'I love you' either, I'd guess."

She shook her head, still not looking at him.

"You've come dangerously close to the L word by calling us lovers, though. After all, 'lovers' contains the L word."

"The L word? I thought the L word was 'lesbian.' At least, the TV show said it was." A smile flickered across her face.

"I assume you have noticed on the occasions when I have been naked with you that I am not eligible to be a lesbian, not without surgical intervention," Leo said.

The smile was now a full-fledged grin. "Yes, I have most definitely noticed."

He pulled the car to the curb in front of his house and cut the engine. With one finger on her chin, he turned her face toward him, and with all the seriousness he could muster, said, "Why's it so bad to think we might turn out to be more than friends?"

"It's not bad; it's scary. Suppose … " She broke off the sentence and returned her gaze to the roof of the truck cab, every muscle in her face tense.

"Suppose … what? Suppose it doesn't work out? Suppose it's not real? Suppose I turn out to be the advance scout for the zombie apocalypse?"

He thought he could see her face relax.

"I don't think you're any more a zombie than you are a lesbian."

"I'm relieved. So what's the 'suppose' factor?"

"When I look around, I see a lot of failed relationships. I mean, look how it turned out for my mom."

"Your father really did a number on you, didn't he?"

"More like on my mom."

"He may have left your mom, but he did a number on you both." Leo slid toward her and collected her into his arms. "I'm sorry for what happened to you and your mom. But you're not your mom and I'm not your dad." He kissed the side of her head. "If we go inside where there are more comfortable places to sit than on the gearshift and hand brake, I'll continue trying to convince you I'm trustworthy."

She laughed. "If there's one thing I know about you, it's that you're trustworthy. But going inside is a good idea. Walter's waiting for us."

• • •

The following day, Leo and Shannon spent hours packing up dozens of thin glass tubes of varying colors, sizes and shapes, securing them in the back of Leo's pickup truck and transporting them to Vancouver where they schlepped them from the truck to the small bedroom Shannon used as a home office. By the time they were finished, the shelves along one side of the room were stacked with glass and Shannon's books were piled on the floor.

Leo was right. Amanda was effusive in her thanks. She'd kissed and hugged Shannon when the GlassCo office was clear of the pieces. Now there was space for the other two studio mates to store the work they were creating for their shows at the end of the summer.

After the last load of glass was safely stored in Shannon's house, Leo left to go home and Shannon took a walk around the Historic Reserve. It was a lovely evening; it had been another wonderful weekend. Well, except for Friday's dinner which she'd managed to forget for the past two days because being with Leo wiped most every bad thing from her mind. Just as being at his house had removed the worry about either her father or Jeremy showing up at her house. When she finally got up the nerve to check her phone, neither had called, texted, or emailed. She was safe.

For the moment.

• • •

The moment ended on Monday afternoon when her father showed up at work. Shannon was beginning to wonder if there was a sign she'd missed on the front of city hall saying, The door is always open to anyone who wants to hassle Shannon Morgan.

Marty Morgan smiled and said, "Knock, knock" then walked into her cubicle without waiting for an invitation. He plopped down on the chair beside her desk and said, "We didn't leave things on a very good footing on Friday. I'm sorry about that. Mostly because we need to get some things straightened out."

"Hello to you, too, Daddy. And please, feel free to interrupt me at my workplace anytime you want. I have no responsibilities other than dealing with you."

"If I thought you'd return a phone call or an email, I might not have to drop in like this. But you'd ignore them, wouldn't you?"

"You don't know my phone number or email address."

"Jeremy gave them to me. Answer my question about whether you'd respond if I'd tried to use them."

"I don't honestly know, Daddy. You made me angry on Friday ambushing me the way you did. I mean, in spite of the fact I only see you every couple of years when you bounce in and out of my life like a basketball, you seem to think you know what's best for me."

"I don't think that, sweetheart. I just want my daughter to be happy. And to try and forgive her old dad for not always being around. It was your grandfather's last wish that we get this sorted out between us."

"If his death was so sudden, how come you know what his last wish was?"

"Well, not his *last* last wish. His last wish that he told me about. When I talked to him the last time." He shifted in the chair and picked up a pencil from her desk, bouncing the eraser end on the arm of the chair. "You know he always loved you. You were his favorite grandchild, just like I was his favorite son."

"You were his only son and I was his only grandchild, Daddy. Don't try that approach to make me feel sorry for you. It won't work."

"Whatever. He wanted us to be closer. He wanted you to be happy. I told him about your friend Jeremy and he was very impressed with what he heard. Said he thought you'd make a good couple."

Shannon closed her eyes and calmed herself. "Let me make it clear. It's over with Jeremy. We dated for a while. He left. I've moved on. I have a new boyfriend. End of story."

"I'm sorry to hear that. I know that Jeremy thinks it could be something else."

"You believe him over your own daughter?" She was beginning to lose it again.

"Not necessarily. But I do recognize when people are making mistakes. I should. I've made enough of them in my life. Jeremy recognizes he made a mistake and wants to make it up. And I don't want you to make the mistake of turning away someone who's good for you."

"I'm not. He isn't." She turned back to her desk, shuffling papers, hoping her father would take the hint.

"Looks like you're trying to tell me the conversation is over. I'm not sure it is, but I'll leave on one condition. I want you to go out to dinner with Louise and me … "

"No. No dinners where I'm bushwhacked. Sorry."

"Let me finish. I want you to go out to dinner with Louise and me—only the three of us—so you can get to know her. She liked you. Said she admired your spirit. We want you to come to Las Vegas when we get married. Be part of the wedding. That's another thing your grandfather wanted—he met Louise a few months back and said he hoped we could all be together at the wedding. I know Louise wants it, too. In fact, I think she wants to talk to you about an idea she has. And remember, I have your inheritance to deliver to you."

Shannon closed her eyes, trying to think of a reason to say no. She couldn't come up with one. But then, that was the story of her life—knowing in her head she should say no when he didn't treat her the way she wanted him to, but saying yes in the hopes that, somehow, he would be different this time. Opening her eyes, she said, "All right. I'll do it, as long as it's only you and Louise. Where and when?"

"You tell me this time."

"Okay, Wednesday night. Right after work. Meet me at the entrance to city hall at five-thirty. We'll have dinner in the restaurant at the Hilton next door."

"It's a date." He stood, leaned over her desk, and kissed her cheek. "Thanks, sweetheart. I knew you wouldn't be cruel to your old dad." With no more good-bye than there had been a hello, he sauntered out of her cubicle, whistling.

Chapter Fifteen

Marty and Louise were waiting for Shannon in the lobby of city hall on Wednesday. Her father kissed her cheek, and much to her surprise, so did Louise.

"I'm so glad we have a chance to do this over," Louise said. "I want to spend a little time with you without all the drama of last Friday."

"Sounds good to me, too, Louise," Shannon responded.

The three walked the block to the restaurant at the hotel where Marty had made reservations. After they had ordered their meals, Louise said, "Okay, now let's do what we should have had a chance to do last week. I'll tell you mine, if you'll tell me yours."

"My what?"

"Your story. All your father said was you were close for a long time, but he hasn't seen much of you since college. Now that I think about it, he hasn't even mentioned where you went to college."

Although she was surprised her father had claimed a closeness that was never there, Shannon didn't want to embarrass him by disputing what he'd told the woman he probably was trying to impress. She let the comment about being close to him go and only responded to the question about her alma mater. "I went to UC Santa Cruz. Majored in politics. I've always loved the subject."

Her father muttered something about how all politicians were corrupt and shouldn't be trusted. Louise's pat on his hand could have been a sign of affection or a signal to hush. Whichever it was, it worked to silence her father.

"How'd you land in Vancouver?" Louise asked, picking up her glass of wine for a sip. Shannon noticed her father had gulped his cocktail down and was signaling to the server for another.

"A classmate told me about a job opening in the mayor's office for a press aide and I applied. I've always loved the Pacific Northwest. Fell in love when my mom and I visited a cousin of hers in Seattle."

"He's a worthless piece of shit," her father said. "He and his equally worthless wife had half a dozen kids who are probably all on welfare now."

Embarrassed for him, Shannon tried to talk over his comment, addressing herself only to Louise. "Anyway, I worked there until this job came up. I'm the community relations and public involvement coordinator. I work on public hearings, deal with homeowner associations, and listen to people complain about dogs and noisy neighbors. This time of the year, I also help manage the annual Fourth of July event."

Their server interrupted with their salads.

When she'd left, her father said, "Sounds like you have a plateful. I didn't realize your job was so responsible."

"You've never asked, Daddy." Shannon stabbed a piece of lettuce with unnecessary force.

"Your job is even more reason for you to think about the kind of man you want to get involved with. You deserve someone who has an equally responsible job. Someone who's a professional. Like Jeremy." Marty had finished his second drink and was signaling for another.

"Daddy, I told you. I'm dating someone else now. He's a wonderful man. I think you'd like him."

Louise intervened before Marty could say anything else. "Tell me about your new man."

"His name is Leo Wilson. He's an artist." She didn't let her father's snort of derision deter her. "We met through work. A local foundation awarded him seventy-five thousand dollars for a glass art installation during the Fourth of July celebration here. I'm in charge of … "

"Seventy five thousand dollars of taxpayer money for art? Where are the priorities of your city?" her father said.

"A private foundation awarded the money, Daddy. No public dollars."

"Still … " He gulped down his third drink. "A man who can't find real work and plays with art isn't exactly the kind of man I want for my daughter."

"I'm smart enough to know the kind of man I want, Daddy, and you … "

Louise intervened again. "How about we limit the conversation topics to you, me, and your dad? And thank you for telling me about yourself, Shannon. Maybe you'd like to know a bit about me."

Shannon took a deep breath, ashamed of letting her father goad her into yet another pointless conversation. She nodded. "Of course. I was about to ask."

"Well, I'm a nurse. I'm divorced with two daughters around your age. They live in Reno, where I live. They're both married, and I have one grandson, a baby named Trey."

"You look too young to be a grandmother," Shannon said. And meant it.

"Thank you. But as much as I'd like to think otherwise, it's undeniably true," Louise said with a shy smile.

"How did you and Daddy meet?"

"It's kind of a funny story. I volunteer at a soup kitchen a couple times a month. One Saturday I was dishing out lunches when this man came up to the serving table and started talking to me. I thought he was a client and I kept trying to give him food. It was Marty. He was there to check on the new computer he'd sold to the group running the shelter where the soup kitchen is."

"I didn't know you were selling computers, Daddy."

"Big market for them. I can hook you up with a good deal if you're interested."

He'd slipped into salesman mode in only seconds. But at least he was trying to sell her a computer not a man this time.

"Anyway," Louise continued, "once we got it all sorted out, he asked me to have coffee with him. That was six months ago and we haven't spent much time apart since."

"How do your daughters feel about … " Shannon paused, not sure how to phrase the rest of the sentence. Finally she said, "about your getting married?"

"They want me to be happy. And Marty makes me happy." Louise smiled at Marty and the grin he gave her in return said a lot to Shannon about how real their relationship was.

"I hope, Marty and I hope," Louise went on, "you and Jennifer and Jessica—my daughters—will be our attendants at our wedding. It would mean a great deal to both of us."

"How thoughtful of you." Shannon took another mouthful of lettuce and chewed for a few minutes before asking, "When exactly is the wedding taking place?"

"We were planning it for the weekend after the Fourth of July."

"The timing may be something of a problem for me. I'll be coming off the big Independence Day event and trying to catch up on what's piled up while I was busy. I'm not sure I can get the time off to fly to Las Vegas for more than an overnight."

An overnight when she'd have to be away from Leo, too, since she was pretty sure he wouldn't be included in the festivities.

"Well, then, we'll have to see about changing the date. It's important you're there and we'd like it to be for more than one night. My daughters are anxious to meet you. How about we see what we can do to move the date to later in the month, maybe the last week?"

"I hate to make you change your plans because of me," Shannon said.

"We're only having a small ceremony in one of the wedding chapels. It's not a problem to move it if it means you'll be there," Louise said.

"Let me know the date and I'll talk to my boss about taking some time off."

The rest of the meal was amicable enough. The tension between Shannon and her father was at a minimum. She was surprised to learn he planned to stay in Vancouver for another week or two, maybe even longer so he could see the Fourth of July event she was in charge of, he said. She had mixed feelings about his plans. Part of her wanted to show him how good she was at her job. Part of her wondered why he was really staying.

By the time dessert—and her father's after dinner drink—arrived, Shannon was close to comfortable with the evening. It was mostly thanks to Louise who was doing her best, it seemed, to keep the conversation on safe topics. Shannon had come to like her very much and to hope this time her father was with a woman who could give him a good life. Maybe even help her finally get closer to him.

She was almost ready to leave when Marty said, "Now, we have one more thing to discuss: your grandfather's will." He motioned to Louise who pulled a package out of the large hobo bag she'd carried. "Here's the first part." Handing the package to Shannon, he smiled and looked expectantly at her.

Shannon untied the string and removed the brown paper wrapping. It was an odd way to present what was inside—a long strand of what she knew were real pearls, a diamond engagement ring, and a gold bangle bracelet she remembered from family stories that she'd teethed on.

She could feel tears build up and reached for her own purse to grab a tissue. When she had wiped her eyes and blown her nose, she fumbled for her father's hand. "Thank you, Daddy. You don't know how much this means to me. I remember Gramma wearing all these pieces. She was so special. And I love it that Granddad thought to leave them to me."

"Well, you know how much he loved you. He may have been old but there was nothing wrong with his mind." He brought out a wallet from the inside pocket of his jacket. "There's one more thing: he left you some money. It's not much. The bulk of his estate came to me. But it might help you buy a house or something."

The check was for ten thousand dollars and would go a long way to paying for her college courses. "That's more than I expected. I had no idea he had that much money."

"He saved all of his life and invested well." Marty shrugged his shoulders and broke eye contact. "Better than I have, anyway." Louise patted his hand, and he seemed to brush off the mood. "There was quite a bit of money in the end."

"I'm happy for you, Daddy. It'll give you a good start on your new life with Louise."

"Yes, well, there are a few things that have to get taken care of first, but I think it'll be okay." He smiled across the table. "Everything will be just fine if you promise to be at the wedding."

It was an odd change of subject, but Shannon wasn't going to press it. Her father seemed much more mellow now and she didn't want to rock the boat. "I can't promise anything yet, Daddy, but I'll try. I'll talk to my boss on Monday and see what I can do."

"We really need you there, don't we, honeybun?" He patted Louise's hand, which Shannon was beginning to believe was some sort of calming signal they used between them.

"Absolutely, we want you there. But most importantly, we want you to *want* to be there with us to share the day."

The evening ended with Louise and Marty walking her home. Pointing out the historic highlights along the way gave her a safe topic of discussion. They both kissed her good night on her front porch and left.

As she watched them walk hand-in-hand back toward the center of town, Shannon tried to shake off the feeling there was more to this than her father was revealing, but she couldn't figure it out. His recent behavior didn't give her much reason to trust him. Hell, his behavior all her life gave her little reason to trust him. And yet, he seemed interested in having her at the wedding more than he had ever wanted her involved in anything before. Was it foolish of her to hope that this was the change in his attitude she'd always wanted? Maybe his relationship with Louise and her relationship with her daughters had opened his eyes.

She was tired. It was all too complicated for her to think about any more. She turned out the lights, headed upstairs, and collapsed into bed, not even bothering to floss.

• • •

Two nights after the dinner with her father, Leo and Shannon split their weekend together between Vancouver and Portland. The Vancouver half was dinner at her house with Powell and her latest hunky guy on Saturday night. The Portland piece was a Sunday brunch with some of Leo's family at his sister's house.

Dinner with Powell was nothing but laughter and stories as Powell flirted outrageously with both her date and Leo and told embarrassing stories about her friend. There was the time Shannon called the governor of Washington by his predecessor's name—a predecessor who happened to be his worst political enemy. And the time she scheduled a public meeting to discuss cultural sensitivity on the holiest day in the Muslim calendar. She was about to launch into another one when Shannon cut her off by bringing out dessert.

Brunch with Leo's family was equally delightful. His sister Olivia Wilson lived in Sellwood, south of Portland, with her wife, Tanya Jefferson. They had been together as a couple for a decade but had only been able to marry recently when Washington State passed the marriage equality law. They had two daughters, Chloe and Alyssa. Leo told her on the way there how each of the women had carried and given birth to one daughter. The two women and their daughters were the most beautiful family Shannon could remember. Olivia had contributed the Wilson family's startling blue eyes to one daughter; Tanya had passed on her brown eyes to the other. But the best part was the caramel and latte skin color of the two little girls, mid-way between Olivia's Caucasian skin and Tanya's African-American color.

In addition to the Wilson-Jefferson family, one of the Wilson brothers was there with his son and daughter for a short visit before he went to the airport to pick up his wife, who was returning from a trip to see an ailing parent. Leo's mother and father, who insisted she call them Bill and Kate, made up the rest of the brunch party. They were obviously doting grandparents and spent most of the time before brunch visiting with the children.

As they ate eggs Benedict and fresh fruit and drank perfectly brewed coffee, the elder Wilsons asked Shannon some of the same things Louise had asked her on Wednesday, and she found herself repeating her "story."

Then Olivia asked her to tell them what her brother was up to. At the time she asked, Leo was playing with Shannon's knee under the table, so the question had several layers of meaning.

Shannon choked on her glass of juice and saw Leo smirk before he patted her on the back.

When she had the coughing under control, she said, "You mean his art installation?"

"Of course, what did you think I meant?" It was obvious Olivia knew exactly what Shannon was thinking.

"I can't believe he hasn't been bragging about landing the biggest art grant ever awarded by the Community Foundation," Shannon said. "It'll be a glass art installation like no one has ever seen in the region. Well, except for the big Chihuly exhibit at the art museum a bunch of years back."

"We knew he'd gotten the grant. I think the whole city heard him yelp when he got the news. But he's never told us exactly what he'll be doing." His sister was grinning at Leo from the head of the table. "Why do you think we encouraged him to bring you to brunch? It was the only way we could figure out how to pry the information out of him."

"As always, my sweet sister, you exaggerate," Leo said. "But if you want to hear what I'll be doing, I'd be—"

"Nope," Olivia said. "I want an unbiased observer's opinion on what you're doing. You *are* unbiased, aren't you, Shannon?"

"Are you, Shannon?" Leo asked, his mouth working hard to keep from smiling.

"Well, I guess I can put on my city employee hat and make a few observations."

"Wait," Leo said. "Is this the hat you wore when I first asked you to help me get the permits I needed, or is it the hat you wore after I walked you through the Reserve and wowed you with what I had in mind?"

"There's a story here, isn't there? Did she thwart your plans, baby brother? Did the famous Leo Wilson charm fail at first?"

"Olivia, let Shannon get a word in here," Leo's mother said, although she was laughing as she said it.

Shannon eventually gave a brief description of what Leo planned and everyone stopped laughing long enough to congratulate him on his project and to promise they'd be at the event and take photos.

On the ride home, Shannon thought about the two meals she'd had with their respective families. Her dinner with her distant and emotionally disengaged father was as far removed from brunch with Leo's family as possible. She wasn't sure she'd ever been with a family so close-knit, so warm, so welcoming. It was everything she'd always wanted in a family and had never had.

Having met his family, she understood exactly why Leo was the way he was. Did her family, if you could call it that, explain who she was in the same way? It worried her. And didn't Leo deserve someone who had a normal family and who could give him the care and attention he had obviously had all his life? The kind of care and attention he knew how to give? The kind she could only dream about?

The difference between their lives wasn't defined by what they did or how much money they earned, despite what her father had suggested. It was explained by where they had come from, how they were raised, and who they were because of their families.

Leo deserved someone who could give that back to him. And Shannon wasn't sure she was that person.

Chapter Sixteen

The countdown for the Fourth of July had begun. Shannon was now officially up to her ears in alligators. Days were long and sleep was minimal.

Local weather forecasters were consulted with as much reverence as the Oracle at Delphi. Grounds maintenance crews worked to groom the grass on the parade grounds to perfection, even though the thousands of visitors on the Fourth would undo all their efforts by the end of the day. Vendors and musical acts were confirmed and reconfirmed. The million and a half questions about when to arrive, where to set up, or how much space there was in which to set up were answered once, twice, sometimes three times.

As hard as Shannon tried to keep her personal life from bleeding into her work life, it wasn't possible. There was Leo, the best of the incursions, who was now as nervous as an expectant father, which in a way he was, awaiting the birth of his artistic baby. And then there was Jeremy who kept sending her little presents at work, like balloon bouquets and cards. She'd also begun to get calls at home with hang-ups as soon as she answered, which she suspected were also from him, although the number was blocked on caller ID. Hard as she tried to ignore it, she was still aware of his presence in Vancouver and his apparent determination to insinuate himself back into her life.

Last, but not least, there was her father. He'd called several times, to say hello, he insisted. Then late one evening when she had straggled home after a twelve-hour day, there he was, sitting on her porch swing. This time, he was alone, not with Louise to act as buffer.

"Daddy, what are you doing here? You should have called. I've had a helluva day, and I'm not really up for company."

"You shouldn't swear, sweetheart. Men don't like women who sound like sailors." He leaned in and pecked her cheek.

"*Helluva* hardly qualifies as sailor-like swearing. Now if I'd said it had been a *fucking* hard day, *that* might make the grade." She unlocked the front door, hoping her use of the f word would make him leave.

It didn't.

"I have to assume you learned such language from your mother. You certainly never got it from me."

She came close to saying "No, I couldn't have gotten it from you. You were never there." But she refrained. Standing in the doorway to her home, she merely said, "What is it you want? I really need to get to bed. I have another long and difficult day tomorrow."

"Can't I come in? Maybe have drink? I came here hoping to give you good news."

Reluctantly, she moved out of the doorway and let him in. "I'm too tired to be social. Tell me what you want and then, please, let me get some sleep." She closed the door behind him.

"Well, Louise and I … "

A loud knock on the door interrupted him.

Shannon hurried to answer it, hoping it was Leo who'd been dropping off supplies for his installation almost every evening.

Instead, when she opened the door she found Jeremy standing there, a determined look on his face.

"Great. Just what I need. Jeremy. What do you want? I'm tired and not up to this tonight."

"One more chance, Shannon. What I want is one more chance. Dinner together. That's it. If you still feel the same way after dinner … "

"I'm too busy right now." But before she could say she really didn't think one more dinner would make a difference anyway, her father came up beside her and welcomed Jeremy with open arms. Literally—he hugged Jeremy.

"Good to see you, my boy. Come on in. You'll be interested in what I was about to tell Shannon." Over his daughter's objections, he waved Jeremy into the living room and closed the door.

"Now I can tell both of you the good news. We've been able to reschedule the wedding for the last week in July so everyone we want in attendance can be there. I assume you've asked your boss about time off, Shannon."

"Not yet. I wanted to make sure it was on before I asked."

"It's on. And you can get time off from work can't you, Jeremy?"

"I'm completely at your disposal, Marty. My work won't stand in the way," Jeremy said.

Shannon glared at her father. "What do you mean, can Jeremy get off from work? Why would his work schedule matter?"

"I want him to travel with you. I don't like the idea of your being alone. He'll be good company."

"I don't need company on a two hour flight to Las Vegas."

"But it's always nice to have a companion and if you drive … "

"That's enough, Daddy. I'm not a child. And you." She turned to Jeremy. "Did your old firm really welcome you back with open arms when you disappeared for over a year with no notice? Or was it only me you didn't let in on your plans?"

Jeremy shrugged his shoulders in what seemed to be an attempt to brush off her question. But she continued to stare at him, eyes narrowed and lips thinned.

"Okay," he admitted, "we haven't exactly come to terms yet on things like title and salary and when I start, but we're in negotiations and I'll make sure I'm free to travel at the end of July."

"And I want him there to be with you," her father repeated.

"This is insane. Why does it matter so much to you? Jeremy has never been important to you before. *I've* never been this important to you before."

"You're wrong. You've always mattered. And it was important to your grandfather that you be at my wedding."

"Granddad's not here. And he knew how hurt I was about you not being part of my life."

"Which is why he wanted you at the wedding. And I want you to be safe, which is why I want Jeremy to make sure you get there. For your safety, I mean."

"You're not listening to me. I'm not interested in spending time with Jeremy. I'm seeing Leo. And, you …" She poked her ex-boyfriend. "Why would you want to be someplace you're not wanted? At least by me."

Jeremy ignored both her poking and most of her questions, responding only to the last one. "It matters to your father, Shannon, so it matters to me. The marriage is the most important thing I can think of right now. And it's the perfect way for us to be together. I wasn't sure I'd get a chance like this but since I have, I'm not turning it down."

"Good man," Marty said. "I knew I recognized you as someone who'd acknowledge when he made a mistake and own up to it. Makes you a better man. One I'd be happy having in my family. We'll get this time off issue settled so the four of us can have a wonderful time in Las Vegas with my daughter back in my life again."

• • •

Leo could barely remember the drive from his studio to Vancouver, so intent was he on mentally going over, yet again, his plans for the days before the Fourth. The days during which the most important installation of his life would take shape. Days starting soon.

He regretted having to give up time alone with Shannon, but she understood how important this was for him.

He'd rounded up a crew of four people—Amanda and Giles, Frank, and another buddy from Firehouse Glass—in addition to himself and Shannon. The six of them would assemble and hang the fireworks over a three-day period, staging it so the most inaccessible, and therefore safest from vandalism, pieces would go up first. The last pieces would be the entrance gazebos—they'd go up the morning of the Fourth so no one would have the chance to use them for batting practice. The flower baskets would be removed and placed on the ground so the glass could be seen.

In the back of his truck he had the signs he wanted affixed to the gazebos and the information booth he'd be staffing. They explained the installation and a bit about glass blowing. His librarian sister had done the copy and Amanda had paid for the signs to be made, her gift to him for his big break. As if fronting the money for some of his supplies hadn't been gift enough. At least he'd been able to pay back the initial loan when he got the first check from the foundation.

He'd been slowly moving all the things he needed for putting up the fireworks to Shannon's house. He wasn't sure what he would have done without her, either.

Without her. God, he couldn't imagine his *life* anymore without Shannon. She'd become as important to him as his work, something he'd never felt about any woman. And he was beginning to believe she felt the same. Maybe once this was over, he'd tell her how he felt and he'd know for sure.

He pulled into the parking area behind her home and went round to the front of the house. As he walked up the path to the door, he heard voices inside. Male voices. Two different men's voices. Whose?

Quietly he went up onto the porch and peeked in the front window. Oh, shit, Jeremy and an older man who looked a bit like Shannon—her father. It had to be. He started to barge in, to be Lancelot for his Guinevere, when the conversation he heard stopped him.

He heard Jeremy say, "This marriage is the most important thing I can think of right now, the perfect way for us to be together. I wasn't sure I'd get a chance like this but since I have, I'm not turning it down."

What the fuck? Jeremy was talking about Shannon and a wedding?

When her father spoke, it got worse. "Good man," he said. "I knew I recognized you as someone who'd acknowledge when he made a mistake and own up to it. Makes you a better man. One I'll be happy having in my family. We'll get this time off issue settled so the four of us can have a wonderful time in Las Vegas with my daughter back in my life again."

Without waiting to hear any more, Leo went back down the steps and around to his truck. Shannon and Jeremy in Las Vegas? A wedding? What the fuck? He knew she wanted her father back in her life. Knew she'd put up with a lot of shit so she could try to win him over but how far was too far to get someone to pay attention to you? Was she going to spend the weekend in Las Vegas with Jeremy, a man she said she wanted out of her life? Could he have been so wrong about her?

He remembered as little of the drive back to his house as he did the drive to Shannon's. But this time what distracted him wasn't his work.

...

"Wait one damn minute, Daddy." Shannon couldn't ever remember being so angry in her whole life. "One, I'm not sure I can get time off to go to Las Vegas. Two, even if I can, I won't go if the price is that I have to travel with Jeremy. Three, if this is what it means to have you in my life, I have spent years trying to get something I now realize isn't worth the trouble."

"Don't talk to me like that, young lady. I'm your father."

"You're the man who contributed half my DNA. You're not now nor have you ever been a father to me. I don't need you to start bossing me around now when you've never wanted to be part of my life on a regular basis." She was clenching and unclenching her fists as she spoke, horrified to realize some part of her brain was urging her to break free and use them. "Leo was right. I've done fine by myself. I don't need you to make me whole or happy."

"I do not want to hear his name. He's not good enough for you."

She yelled as loud as she could, "Leo. Leo. Leo. Leo. Leo."

Jeremy grabbed her arm. "Now you're acting crazy, Shannon. Stop it right now."

She shook off Jeremy's hand and pointed to the door like a ham actor in a bad play. "Get out. Both of you. Jeremy, if you set one foot on my porch or send one more lame gift to city hall or text me or call me at work or at home and hang up, I'm taking out a restraining order against you. And Dad, please tell Louise I appreciate how hard she's worked to bring everyone together, but I simply won't be manipulated anymore. I can't be in Las Vegas for your wedding."

"Don't make such a hasty decision, sweetheart." Her father was beginning to sound almost desperate. "Sleep on it. If you don't want Jeremy with you, come alone. But I really want you there. I won't say anything to Louise until you have a chance to think it over."

"I don't need to think it over." Shannon marched to the front door and flung it open. "You have my answer. Now, both of you please leave. I have a lot of work to do tomorrow and I'm exhausted."

To her surprise, they both left with no further argument, although she noticed them talking on the sidewalk in front of her house before they went separately to their cars. There were two anxious faces and four gesturing hands to go with what appeared to be a very intense conversation. She was too tired to wonder what they were talking about.

• • •

Leo couldn't decide if he should call Shannon. As much as he wanted to know exactly what the hell was going on, he wasn't prepared to hear her say she was going to Las Vegas with Jeremy.

On one hand, he couldn't believe the strong and resourceful woman he was halfway—maybe more than halfway—in love with would do something like spend the weekend with a guy just to please a father she hardly knew.

On the other hand, he knew how much she wanted her father in her life. Knew how long she'd been trying to show him what a good daughter she was so he'd stay around for a change instead of leaving. Again.

Finally, after wearing himself out pacing the floor while he worried the question to death, not to mention wearing Walter out because he was following his master, Leo grabbed his cell and punched her number.

"Leo, I'm glad you called. I thought you were going to bring the signs over tonight. I was worried when you didn't show." She sounded like she always did. Even maybe a little happy to hear from him.

He pushed back a little. "Worried? I would think you'd have too much on your plate to worry about me. And I've made other arrangements for the signs."

She didn't respond at first. "Is something wrong?" she finally said.

"What could be wrong?"

"I don't know. That's why I'm asking you."

It was his turn to be silent while he considered how smart it would be to reveal he'd been standing on her porch eavesdropping.

"Leo? Are you okay?"

"Yeah, fine. Great. Everything's fucking awesome." He decided to give her a chance to explain what was going on. "I just thought what with your plans for Las Vegas and the wedding, not to mention convincing your dad you're finally the daughter he wanted, oh, and all the work connected with the Fourth, you'd be really busy for the next week. So I thought I'd make some other arrangements. Maybe set up a couple times when I know you'll be there so I can arrange to have someone get the pieces for my installation. Get them out of your way so you don't have to be involved."

"Las Vegas? The wedding? How did you know about that? Anyway, that's nothing for you to worry about. I did what I needed to do. My dad is finally paying attention, I think. It's all taken care of." She paused for a moment. "There's really nothing more to say about it, so can we change the subject and talk about your glass installation? I thought you were going to come pick up the glass yourself?"

And there it was. The wedding was taken care of and he shouldn't worry. It was all settled the way she wanted it to make her dad understand her. She was headed for Las Vegas with another man, the one her father approved of, so he was finally paying attention.

"Are you still there?"

"Yeah, I'm here. I'll have Giles or one of the guys from Firehouse meet you at your house after work in a couple days. They can get the glass out of your house, and then you won't have to be bothered with it anymore."

"Won't have to be bothered? What do you mean? I thought…"

He hung up before he heard the end of her sentence.

Chapter Seventeen

"Aren't you Little Mary Sunshine this morning?" Powell was standing in the doorway of Shannon's cubicle holding a mug of coffee in each hand. "I came in here to have coffee with you and hear the latest chapter of the love affair of the century and find you with a scowl on your face that could stop the clock in the park. Or start it, since it isn't working again."

"Go away, Powell. I have work to do." Shannon didn't look up from her computer.

"Nope. I won't go away. You obviously need me." She put the two mugs on Shannon's desk then swung Shannon's chair around to face her. "What's going on? Jeremy the joke-of-a-man still riding your ass, so to speak?"

"I told him if he kept bothering me, I'd be going for a restraining order. I think he took it seriously."

"About damn time. So he's gone. How about your carbon-based-life-form sperm donor?"

"My father? I told him last night I'm through trying to bend over backwards to get him to be part of my life. It isn't worth the effort. The last straw was when he insisted Jeremy accompany me to his wedding so I wouldn't have to travel alone. He's worried about my safety, he claims."

"Are you going to the wedding?"

"Not now, I'm not. I feel a little guilty because they changed the date so I could attend but not guilty enough to jump through his hoops anymore."

"Bloody well right. After the shit your father has put you through, you shouldn't feel guilty about anything, girlfriend."

"I don't feel guilty about my … about Marty. It's Louise. She seems like such a nice person. Better than he deserves, I'm convinced. Now."

"Write her a letter and apologize." Powell flicked away Shannon's concerns like lint, sat in the visitor's chair, and took a sip of her coffee. "Okay, you gave Jerk-off Jeremy the boot, had a come-to-Jesus moment with Marty—you should be floating on air and grinning like a baboon."

"Yeah, well, after all the drama with Marty and Jeremy, I had a phone call that sucked."

"From whom?" She scanned Shannon's face and seemed to see the answer there. "No, not from Studly-Do-Right?"

"Sadly, yes. He was cool and distant, said I'd have too much to worry about, what with the wedding in Las Vegas and the Fourth, so he wouldn't be bothering me anymore. I tried to tell him I had the Las Vegas thing under control, but he backed off even more. He's sending friends to clear out the glass from my house." She looked up at her friend and could feel the tears backed up in her eyes. "Do you think he was using me to get his damn art installation settled?"

"Bullshit. I saw him with you. The man was in love with—*is* in love with—you. He took you to meet his *family*, for God's sake."

"If he's in love with me, he has a warped way of showing it. I don't understand what all this backing away is about."

"I don't know either, but I'm for damn sure going to find out."

"Powell, don't you dare call him."

Powell finished her coffee and stood. "Okay, honey, if that's what you want. I won't call him. I promise." Walking to the door, she threw back over her shoulder, "Men. Can't live without them. Can't kill them when they act like assholes."

• • •

Leo had decided the only way to get through the next few days was to throw himself into his work. Handling hot glass required focus and concentration, which should keep his mind off Shannon and what he'd heard about her plans.

Unfortunately, it wasn't working so well. After he'd screwed up two pieces he was trying to create with Giles's help, he fled to Vancouver to his friends at Firehouse Glass. There he was confining his efforts to creating a few more fireworks pieces he wanted to have in reserve in case he needed them.

He wasn't doing much better in Vancouver. Not when Shannon's presence only two blocks away at city hall was as alluring as a siren's song. He was about to give up and go home when the back door to the hot shop was jerked open, letting in cooler air than he was comfortable with, given he was about to bring a piece out of the heat.

Without looking, he yelled, "Hey, whoever opened the door, close it. I don't want this piece to thermoshock."

"I don't give a flying fuck what you want. I'm here to talk to you," a woman's voice said. "Put down the damn glass so I can."

It was Shannon's friend Powell, and she sounded pissed as hell. She was dressed in business clothes but the expression on her face wasn't the least bit businesslike. Unless the business was the revenge of the Borg.

"Powell? What're you doing here?" Leo asked.

"Want me to get her out of here?" his friend Frank asked.

"No, I'll talk to her. But first, shut the door, please, so I can get this piece out and into the annealing oven."

When that was accomplished, he motioned Powell out of the hot shop and into the front retail area. Only open by appointment, it was deserted.

"Okay," he said, stretching out the word, "what's so important you had to interrupt my work?"

"Take the glasses off so I can see your eyes," she demanded.

When he'd complied, she said, "So, I interrupted your goddam work, did I? The hell with your work. Because of your *work*, the almighty god Art, you thought it was perfectly all right to screw over one of the nicest people I've ever met, didn't you? Anything to get your *work* in front of people. Anything to …"

"What the hell are you talking about?"

"You could have just taken her out to lunch, showed her around the parade grounds. You could have given her a diagram of what you were planning so she knew who to contact for the permissions. You didn't have to fuck her. But, no, you had to go the extra mile, make yourself irresistible, use your charm to make sure …"

"You think I seduced Shannon to get my permits issued? What kind of asshat do you think I am?"

"Good. At least you're bright enough to figure out what I think of you. I don't have to be more explicit." She was shaking her finger at him as if he were an errant schoolboy and she the teacher who found him out. "You hurt her, and so help me God you are going to pay for it. I don't know how, I don't know when, but I will make sure—"

"*I* hurt *her*? By what, falling for her before I found out she was about to run away for a weekend in Las Vegas with some jerk she doesn't love so she can make her father happy? How am I the one who did the hurting? I'm not to blame for whatever hurt there is. She's the one."

"Running away with some jerk? Pleasing her father? What are you talking about?" The *schoolteacher* now looked more confused than angry.

Leo forked his fingers through his hair and sighed. "Okay, look, this isn't the easiest thing to cop to, but I overheard a conversation she had last night with her father and Jeremy. I was bringing some stuff for the installation to her house, and they were so loud they didn't hear me walk up the steps to the porch."

"So you eavesdropped."

"Yeah. Good thing I did, too. Otherwise I'd never have known about the plans to go to Las Vegas with Jeremy." He tried hard to keep the hurt off his face. "Jeremy was crowing about how important the wedding was to him and how grateful he was to get a second chance. Her father was really happy about it, too. Talked about all the fun the four of them would be having now that he and Shannon were reconciled. About how great it'll be to have Jeremy in the family. I guess she finally has what she wants—her father accepts her as long as she's with Jeremy."

By now there was a smile—or a smirk—trying to tip up the corners of Powell's mouth. "So, when you heard what Marty and Jeremy said, you, what, waited to hear what Shannon thought, so you could understand what was going on?" She waved her hand dismissively. "No, don't tell me. Let me guess. You stomped down the steps and went home and sulked."

"I didn't stomp and I didn't sulk. I did go home. And I called Shannon later to give her a chance to explain herself. She sure as hell didn't say much about it until I brought it up, and then all she said was she had Las Vegas under control."

"Ah, so you missed the part where she told Jeremy if he didn't leave her alone, she was getting a restraining order. And the part where she told her dad she was through trying to please him because it wasn't worth the effort."

"She … what? I don't understand. I know what I heard. Jeremy was talking about a wedding and going with Shannon to Las Vegas."

Powell rolled her eyes. "Jesus, men are idiots. If you're going to eavesdrop, for crissake, pay attention. Marty and Louise changed the date of their wedding so Shannon could be part of it. *That's* what Marty was there to tell her. Then he fucked up big time by insisting that Jeremy accompany Shannon to Vegas. Shannon told him to take his wedding and shove it up his ass—only she was probably a lot nicer about it—and threw both of them out."

"You're making this up." She had to be. He knew what he'd heard. He couldn't be mistaken. Or could he? What if he was wrong and Powell was right? A faint ray of optimism began to break through the black cloud he'd carried over his head all day.

"Sunshine, what would be the point of making up a story when the truth is so much more interesting?"

"I don't know. After last night, nothing makes much sense, so why would your coming here be any different?"

"Lucky for you I'm here to help. Now I can get this all straightened out with Shannon and—"

"Don't tell her anything. Please. I'm not hiding behind you. I got myself into this jam; I have to get myself out." He was pacing the floor again. "Does she have a meeting or anything tonight?"

"No, she's off at the regular time."

"Then I'll go see her and throw myself on her mercy."

"I'm not sure there's much mercy to throw yourself on. She's a little short of it right now. Particularly when it comes to men."

"Guess I can't blame her. Me, her ex, her father. Lucky she has you."

"You bet your sweet ass she's lucky to have me. And if you're with her, you get me, too. Don't you forget it."

"You're not likely to let me, are you?"

• • •

For the rest of the afternoon, Leo hung around Firehouse Glass making more firework pieces he was sure he didn't need to keep himself busy until the end of Shannon's work day. Somehow, knowing he would have the chance to get it all worked out with her in a few hours was soothing. He was able to focus on the work. As a result, he produced some of the best pieces yet. He even created a new design, making curly pieces of bright yellow to mimic the effect in some fireworks of the center going off in crazy circles when the shell was exploded.

By the time his buddies were ready to close up the hot shop, he was relaxed and eager to do his *mea culpa* and see how forgiving Shannon was. He didn't have fresh clothes to swap for the old jeans and T-shirt he wore, but he cleaned up the best he could and went out into the late June night to drive the few short blocks to Shannon's place.

His bubble of happiness deflated as he approached her house. By the time he got to the parking lot in back, he had more questions than confidence. Suppose she wasn't home? Suppose she saw who it was and wouldn't open the door? Suppose she was so pissed off she wouldn't let him explain? What then?

When he walked from the parking lot to the front of her house, he could see the light in her living room she always turned on as soon as she got home. So, question one was answered. She was there. Now all he had to do was walk a few more paces along the sidewalk and up the steps to her porch and he'd know the answer to question two. The third answer, the really important one, would quickly follow.

He knocked. No answer. Knocked again. Finally the door opened, and before she even spoke, he could see how stone cold angry Shannon was.

"What are you doing here? I thought you were sending friends to pick up your work," she said. The edge in her voice could have etched glass.

Not exactly the warm welcome he'd gotten before, but then he deserved this he supposed. "I … ah … was but I decided I'd come myself, maybe talk to you, explain … "

"There's really nothing you could explain I want to hear." She opened the door fully and motioned him into the house. "You know where the glass is. Why don't you go get it?"

"Can't I talk to you for a minute before I do? I have to explain … "

"I'm sick and bloody tired of men trying to *explain* their behavior to me. You were clear enough last night on the phone about how pissed you are at me. Or how through with me you are. Whatever. I got the message. Now get your glass." She stalked to the kitchen, which was hardly far enough to make a dramatic exit but left him standing at the door with no other option than to go retrieve his glass.

He trudged up the steps to the second floor. The office where he'd stored his work was between her bedroom and the bathroom. From one room came the flowery scent that made him think of nuzzling her neck and hearing her make little noises of contentment. The other made him think about the nights he'd spent in her bed, loving her, her body so responsive to his, her mouth so hot, so wet.

He shouldn't go there, had to block the images flooding his mind so he could focus on the task at hand. Then, after he'd gotten it, he'd try again to apologize. After he'd thrown himself on her mercy, she'd forgive him and they'd both go out to the parade grounds and get the first fireworks installed. At least that's what he wanted.

After four trips, he had the pieces necessary for the first two installations and all the floodlights on Shannon's porch. She'd stayed in her living room as he came and went, ostensibly reading a book, although he noticed she didn't seem to be making much headway with it, which gave him some comfort. She wasn't any more able to focus than he was. Maybe she still had feelings other than anger for him.

When he was finished, he stood in front of her and waited for her to look up from the book he didn't think she was reading. She didn't, even when he coughed dramatically, so he plunged ahead. "You said you wanted to help with the installation. Are you still interested?"

"Excuse me?" Her voice was about as cool as he'd ever heard a woman's voice.

"You said you might want to help. Last week. And I wondered …"

"Last week was last week and this is now. Why would I want to help you?"

"Shannon, if you'll listen to me, let me explain. Please."

"Explain what? What a fool I was to fall for what even your sister called your legendary charm? How I got used by a master? I don't need to hear an explanation of that. I already know."

"Please. I made a mistake when I talked to you last night."

"You sure as hell did." She went to the front door. "Now, if you're finished for the moment, you need to leave."

He followed her, tried to touch her. She recoiled as if struck. "Don't. Just leave."

He looked at her long and hard, finally sighed, and went out the door. "Either I or someone else will be back for the rest of the glass tomorrow night."

"I expect I'll be here then."

"Good-night, Shannon."

"Good-bye, Leo." She slammed the door.

He loaded all the glass and the spots into his truck. Taking one more look back at her house he muttered, "Well, Wilson, fucked up again. Now what?"

Chapter Eighteen

Shannon worried all day about the possibility of facing Leo again, almost deciding not to leave work until late in the hope she'd miss him. But if she wasn't home as she'd promised, he couldn't get the installation up and she'd risk making him fail. She reluctantly admitted she'd have to be there. Keeping her word won in the end.

Powell was weird all day, too, asking her several times how Leo's glass installation was going. Leo, not Studly-Do-Right. Shannon couldn't figure it out. Usually, once Powell had nicknamed a person, it stuck for life. And then there was the smirking. Each time she asked, Powell wouldn't tell her why, but she smirked, as if she knew something Shannon didn't. It was her friend at her most annoying.

The only good part of the day was the phone call from her father saying he was sorry for their misunderstanding and hoped she'd change her mind. He and Louise would be around for a few more days but he wouldn't be contacting her again until he heard from her. She was noncommittal in her response.

It was a relief to see Giles instead of Leo when she opened the door after dinner for the glass pickup. He chatted with her as if he had no idea what had happened between Leo and her. She didn't have the nerve to ask him what he knew. Besides, he was a guy. How much would he have gotten out of Leo other than "Yeah, we broke up." Or something similar.

Broke up. Really? Did they break up? It felt even worse when she thought about it that way. Somehow it was easier to think about it as Leo being a jerk for some unknown reason.

Either way, the result was the same. He wasn't with her anymore and she felt crappy about it.

Giles did tell her they'd gotten two of the fireworks installed and all the lights placed during the day. They expected to get four more fireworks installed the next day. The four remaining displays on the parade grounds would go up the day after and the three cupola installations would go up on the Fourth.

After he left, she tried to beat her curiosity into submission but she couldn't. The urge to see the first fireworks was too much to resist. She had to go see what they looked like.

What they looked like was magic.

Leo's vision for the fireworks had been interesting—a series of glass fireworks in vibrant colors high in the trees and structures around the parade grounds. But the reality was beyond stunning. If this didn't get him the notice he deserved, she didn't know what would. Even in the dusky light and without spotlights on them, the two fireworks, installed in the trees near the National Park visitor center, were amazing.

They were hung at a slight angle so the observer could look up into the center of the piece, just as he or she would with an actual firework. There was an outside ring of thin, slightly curved glass tubes and then smaller inner rings with a center of bright white and pale yellow, as if it were the intense energy of the real thing. One was in shades of blue. The other shades of yellow with the ring closest to the center made of curly pieces. They were so alive looking she half expected the curls to spiral down to earth before dissipating into the night. The two pieces were hung one above the other, the blue one with more curved outside pieces above the yellow one, as if it had been set off first and the sparks were already beginning to fall to earth before the second one had exploded.

It brought tears to her eyes to see them. This was everything Leo said it would be and more. When he'd hung the rest and with the light he'd programmed to go on and off flashing across them, it would be a startling effect, preparing the crowd for the real thing. Rivaling the *real thing* in beauty and power. He was an amazing artist.

He was an amazing man. An amazing lover. She missed him. No, wait, she couldn't miss him; she hated him. Well, not hated. Didn't like. Maybe had been hurt by him. Exactly. He'd hurt her. She tried to keep the thought at the front of her mind as she walked across the parade grounds to her house.

She couldn't. All she could do was miss him.

• • •

On nice days, Shannon walked to work. It combined transportation and exercise and made her feel smug about not adding her car's emissions to air pollution. Today was one of those days when it was not only good policy but also a complete joy. The sun was bright; shadows from the leaves on the old trees lining the street dappled the sidewalks. The preparations for the Fourth were clearly underway from the looks of the stage being set up. She stopped by the split rail fence to watch the workers hoisting the frame for the canvas, which would protect the main stage.

Glancing around, something seemed odd, out of place from the last time she'd walked by. It took a few minutes until she realized what was different. All the lights Leo had set up for his installation were gone. She climbed over the fence and asked the workers if they'd moved them for some reason. They hadn't. She looked around a bit more but couldn't find any trace of them.

She called her office to report what had happened and said she'd be in late while she sorted it out. Then she called Leo.

"Shannon, I'm so glad you called. Can we … ?"

"Leo," she interrupted. "Did you come over here last night and move your spots around? Or did Giles come back after he picked up the glass?"

"The spots? That's why you called?"

"Yes, I'm at the parade grounds now and I don't see them where they were last night when I … where they were last night. Did you move them?"

There was a slight pause and then a sigh. "No, I didn't move them. Why would I?"

"I don't know why you do a lot of things. But the point is, they're not here. I've been all over the parade grounds, and I can't find evidence of them anyplace."

"Has anyone else been working on the grounds?" Leo asked.

"Yeah, the city maintenance crews are here putting up the main stage."

"Maybe they … "

"I asked them. They haven't seen them, much less moved them."

"Okay. We're on our way over to put up the next set of glass. I'll take a look." He paused again. "Will you be there?"

"No, I'm on my way into the office. If you find them, let me know, will you?"

"Yeah, sure. I'll let you know."

And he was gone, leaving Shannon missing him again.

●●●

The day dragged. And when she walked home, what Shannon saw on the parade grounds made the day worse. Leo was still there working. Well, not exactly working. He was showing off the installation to someone. She didn't recognize who at first, but when she got closer, she saw the red hair and the stunning body and realized it was Cathy, his ex. He was showing off his work and she was hanging on his words. Or, more accurately, she was hanging onto Leo. And he didn't seem to mind.

It hadn't taken him long to get back together with her. Or Cathy hadn't taken long to latch onto him again now that he was about to get some publicity for his work. Either way, they certainly looked friendly.

The evening dragged as much as the day had. She was really glad it was Giles who came to take the remaining glass pieces and not Leo. She wasn't sure she could face him. Not yet. Maybe not ever, but certainly not yet.

When Giles left, Shannon went upstairs to put the books back on the shelves where the glass had been. But she couldn't. All she could think about was how much fun she'd had with Leo protecting the glass in blankets, bubble wrap, and big sheets of paper and then carrying them up the steps, kissing when they met in the middle of the steps, one going up, the other going down. Then, when all the glass was safely stored, making love.

They'd made love a lot while they were together—on her desk, in the shower, in bed. There was hardly a horizontal surface where they hadn't made love, not to mention one or two vertical surfaces as well. And, yes, it was making love. Not just sex. Had it ever been just sex? No matter how she'd tried to keep it that way, it had never been just about the chemistry. Not with Leo. It had always been about a connection that was emotional and mental as well as physical.

She had been so sure he loved her. Was sure now she loved him. She still couldn't figure out what had gone wrong. It was killing her. Luckily after the Fourth, she'd never have to see him again.

Never have to see him again. Like that was what she wanted.

Vowing to forget Leo and ignore his work, she settled into her couch with a glass of lemonade and a book. But no matter how much she pretended, she really did want to see what he'd accomplished. So, about nine, before she lost all the light, she gave in and went across the street to see the new pieces.

Even before she got to the trees, a slight tinkling of the glass pieces announced their presence as a gentle breeze moved through them. Walking from tree to tree, she inspected the newly installed fireworks. They were, of course, beautiful. A red, white, and blue pinwheel shape vied with a starburst of vivid pinks streaked in white as her favorite. Or, maybe the brilliant yellow one was her favorite. No, the second blue one. They were all so beautiful they brought tears to her eyes, and she wasn't sure if it was because of what she saw or what she'd lost.

Still unsettled when she climbed into bed, her sleep was restless, with dreams of Leo, some of which woke her up crying. And she kept hearing noises. Backfires, they sounded like. Her neighbors were unusually noisy, too, clomping around on the porch. When her alarm went off the next morning, she felt like she'd been awake all night. It was a hell of a way to start another long workday.

A loud knock at the door interrupted her breakfast. Not expecting anyone so early in the morning, she peeked out her window before she answered. It was the maintenance crew chief.

"Sorry to disturb you, Shannon, but there's something I think you need to see," he said.

"What is it, Ed?"

"Come across to the parade grounds with me. And bring your phone. You might want a photo of it."

She grabbed her phone and keys, and her curiosity piqued both by what he said and the worried look on his face, followed him across the street.

He led her to the trees around the visitor center and showed her what appeared to be piles of trash. Broken bottles, maybe.

"I don't understand. What is this?" Shannon asked.

He pointed up. "Look up."

What she saw almost buckled her knees. The fireworks she'd seen only the night before were hanging like tattered shreds of fabric. "What the hell happened? They couldn't possibly have fallen. Leo—the artist—knew what he was doing when he installed them."

"No, if they'd been improperly installed, I'd imagine the whole thing would've come crashing down. Only part of it was destroyed."

"This is terrible. How?" She kicked at the shattered glass on the ground, then looked up again. "I don't understand."

"Yeah, I don't know why someone would do this either," Ed said.

"No, I mean I don't understand how someone could reach them."

"Big ladder. Rocks. Gun."

"A gun. Oh, God … those weren't backfires I heard last night. They were gunshots."

"There you are. You better hang around to talk to the cops when they get here. I've called them."

"I'll be here. And I'll call the artist. Thanks, Ed."

"Sorry to have to give you bad news to start your day."

As the crew chief walked off, Shannon saw two police cruisers coming down Evergreen Boulevard. When they exited their vehicles, she waved them over to where she was, told them what she knew, and then made a difficult call.

"Leo," she began as the tears she'd been trying to control broke through. "Oh, Leo, I don't know how to tell you."

"What's wrong, Shannon? What happened? Are you all right?"

"I'm okay. But … " A fresh burst of crying stopped her.

"You're not okay. Where are you? I'll be right there."

"Wait. Yes, you have to come over here, to the parade grounds. But you need to know something before you get here." She gulped back more tears. "Your work. Your fireworks installation. Someone destroyed almost all of them last night. The pieces are shattered. Shot."

"Fuck. Goddamn. Son of a bitch," he yelled, his voice tight with anger. Then he was silent for a long moment. Finally he said, "I'll be right there. Don't move."

Shannon was watching the police do a grid search to see if they could find evidence of what had been used to damage the glass when a familiar truck pulled into the parking area across from the Grant House. She didn't know how he'd gotten over to Vancouver so fast. However it was, he got out of the truck at the same speed, vaulting over the fence before the engine died, she swore. She ran to meet him.

"It's horrible. How could anyone be so cruel and destructive? All your work … " She was crying again.

Leo circled her with his arms and pulled her close to him. "Was anyone hurt?"

"No one was around. It apparently happened late last night. When I was over looking at them a little before nine everything was fine. The maintenance crew found the damage when they arrived at seven this morning. I heard what I thought were backfires late last night. It could be that's when they were shot out." She stopped, realizing she was babbling as well as crying.

He kissed the top of her head. "Well, at least one person got to see them. Did you like what you saw?"

She looked up at him. "Aren't you mad? Or heartbroken? Or something?"

"I'm pissed as hell. It's my worst nightmare come true. But mostly I'm trying to figure out how to reinstall the whole damn thing in two days. After that, I'll get really angry and hit something. Or someone."

"Maybe we'll know who did it by then and you can hit him."

The smile he gave her was small but sweet. "I'm glad you saw them before they were destroyed. And I'm glad you called me. Maybe even glad you're doing the crying for me."

She stayed away from the emotional trap he seemed to be laying for her and went with the first part of what he said. "You can reinstall it all? I thought … "

"I made a ton of extra pieces in case I broke some while I was installing it or didn't like the way the pieces were fitting together. I think I have enough glass to get it done. Question is, do I have enough time to get it back up after we clean up the mess."

"And after the cops let you," she added.

"Right. The cops. I guess I better go talk to them and find out," Leo said.

"I don't know how they deal with vandalism like this. It's not exactly a major crime scene. But I wanted them to see what had happened so I could get them to patrol around here for the next couple of nights to make sure it doesn't happen again."

The police assured Leo he could be back at work by the end of the day. And they promised Shannon they'd be patrolling the area carefully for the next few days, but they suggested she find some extra eyes to keep watch. Maybe, they suggested, get her neighbors on Officers' Row to help.

"Maybe I should be the extra eyes," Leo said. "Do you think your neighbors would mind having me outside on the grounds watching all night?"

Shannon spoke without thinking. "I have a better idea. Why don't we both stay up and watch from my porch. That way, we'll be in the shadows and if the vandal returns, he won't know he's being watched."

"He?"

"All right, he or she. Other than my political correctness error, does that work for you?"

"What time shall I show up?"

• • •

She must have looked a wreck when she got to work because everyone from the receptionist to her boss to Powell asked her what was wrong. And quite a few people, her boss included, volunteered to help Leo get the installation back up. She was almost sorry Randy Andy had been so concerned. She'd had him at the top of her list of possible perps. Even after the budget went through with her job safe, she was afraid he would keep trying to make her look bad. And what says failure quite as blatantly as tens of thousands of dollars worth of an art installation in shards on the ground?

However, he seemed genuinely concerned. She questioned his motives until she realized he was probably afraid of what the mayor and city council would think of his department if such a disaster happened on his watch. So his commitment to getting the situation taken care of began to make sense—he was covering his ass. And to help, he recruited other people in the department.

So, thanks to Randy Andy, when Leo called early that afternoon to say the police had released the site so he could begin the reinstallation, Shannon was able to give him a long list of people who were willing to take a half-day off and hang glass.

Chapter Nineteen

Between the Community Development staff who volunteered and the half dozen artist friends who showed up, Leo had quite a crew of assistants. The glass blowers knew how to handle the pieces of glass, and using Leo's sketches, easily put the fireworks together. The city employees got the broken pieces cleaned up using a couple industrial-size vacuums, so even the smallest bits were sucked up, ensuring the crowds of people who'd soon be roaming the parade grounds would be safe.

When the new fireworks were assembled, Shannon's colleagues brought in a bucket truck with a lift on it borrowed from the headquarters of the nearby public utility. It got Leo into the trees more efficiently—and more safely—than he'd been able to do with the extra long extension ladders he'd used initially to hang his work. While he was doing the final installation, the rest of his crew positioned the spotlights Leo had brought to replace those stolen two nights before.

By the time it was too dark to work any longer, all the broken fireworks were replaced, the lights had been realigned, and Leo was back on schedule. He offered to buy drinks at the Grant House to thank everyone but was turned down in favor of a rain check.

Actually, he was glad they didn't take him up on his offer. He needed time to pack up his supplies and a chance to consider what he was about to do: spend the night with Shannon on her porch. It was close to ten o'clock, which meant eight hours until the sun came up. Eight hours of sitting in the dark with her. Come to think of it, he felt like he'd been fumbling around in the dark with her for a couple days already.

Let's see—how many misunderstandings and missteps had there been between them? First he was sure she was about to run away to Las Vegas with Jeremy to please her father. Then, when he found out how wrong he was, she wasn't receptive to his clumsy attempt to explain. Next, he'd been waiting for her to come home from work the day before so he could try to explain again and Cathy showed up. Leo was pretty sure Shannon had seen him with her, which might have led her to think he was seeing his old girlfriend.

But this morning, she'd seemed more upset by what happened than he was. She'd let him comfort her, hold her, even sneak a kiss on the top of her head. That was the last of the conflicting signals he could think of, none of which he understood.

He was about to spend the night with her. Not in her bed or his but on the porch. In the dark. They'd started out sitting on the porch swing the first time he'd really kissed her, and now they were back there. The circle was complete.

What did it mean that she'd invited him? Was it a good sign? A bad sign? Not a sign at all?

It was time to find out. He made a quick phone call then started toward Shannon's house.

• • •

Shannon didn't know what had come over her. With still no idea of what had happened between them the past week, she'd asked Leo to watch for the vandal from her porch. With her. She didn't know whether he thought of her as anything other than a means to an end, or whether he was back with his old girlfriend, or what it had meant when he'd immediately held her and even kissed her to comfort her when she spas crying. If the list of what she didn't know was long, the list of what she wanted to know was short: what had happened to make him so cold?

She sighed. Sitting in the dark seemed like an appropriate activity for the two of them right now.

From the porch swing, she watched him amble across the parade grounds and cross the street. Even in the dusky night he looked so handsome, so sexy. Not to mention he was smart and talented and funny and could kiss her senseless … oh, crap. She had to stop *that* line of thinking or this would be the longest, most uncomfortable, night of her life.

He took the porch steps two at a time, said hi, and sat at the opposite end of the swing. His arrival was followed by an awkward silence for what seemed like an eternity.

Leo spoke first. "Well, here we are."

She shifted her weight a bit to make sure there was plenty of space between them. "Yup, here we are." Another round of silence. "Maybe I should make a pot of coffee. We might need it to stay awake."

"Let me help." He stood up and extended his hand to her.

"No, it's okay. I can do it myself." Shannon avoided him as she rose, too, and headed inside.

"I know you can. I thought I'd help. To thank you, I mean. You know, for going out of your way for me." He followed close behind her to the kitchen.

She pulled out the container of beans and two mugs. "I want this to go off for the Fourth almost as much as you do."

"Right. Your boss might put your job back on the chopping block if it goes bad. You need to make sure this all works out to impress him." He took the bag of beans and poured some into the grinder.

"My job isn't in danger anymore." She faced him. "I want your installation to be successful because you've worked so hard, put so much of yourself into this. You deserve success."

Leo put his hands on her waist. "I deserve something else, Shannon."

"What do you mean?" She wanted to move away but couldn't. It felt so good to have him touch her again.

"I deserve a chance to explain one or two things to you." He pulled her close to him, close enough to kiss her.

All she could see was his mouth. Oh God, if he kissed her it would all be over. She couldn't possibly resist him if he kissed her. She loved kissing him. Loved the feel of his mouth on hers. She stepped back. "I don't think there's anything you need to explain."

"Yes, there definitely is. But standing here close enough to kiss you, I can't think clearly enough to explain anything. Let's make the coffee and go back on the porch. It'll be easier for me there." He ground the coffee beans and dumped them in the coffeemaker.

Her hand was shaking as she filled the machine with water and started it brewing. He was as disturbed by being close as she was. Did it mean what she hoped it did? Or was it his way of making sure things went off okay for the Fourth? He wouldn't be so manipulative, would he? The Leo she loved wouldn't be, she was sure. But was he that man?

When she was finished with the coffee, he took her hand and led her back to the now dark porch. This time he sat close enough to her to put his arm around her. She wanted to escape his touch but, once again, she couldn't bring herself to back away. Not when having him so close meant she could smell his clean, masculine scent and feel the heat from his body. At least in the dark she couldn't see his mouth, didn't think so much about kissing him, about how his lips felt when he …

He broke into her fantasy. "First, I owe you an apology. A big one. Once I explain why, I'm not sure you're ever going to want to see me again. But if I'm not honest with you, I couldn't live with myself." He drew her against his chest. She couldn't see his face and wondered if maybe that's why he did it.

"Remember when I told you I was going to bring the signs over? Well, I did."

Shannon sat up, scanned his face, tried to see his expression. "But you never came to the house. And when you called, you said you'd made other arrangements."

Leo tried to hold her again but she resisted. Instead, she stared at him until he cleared his throat then spoke again. "I did come to your house. I was about to knock on the door when I heard voices inside. Men's voices."

"My father and … " She dropped her gaze. "And Jeremy. You heard Jeremy."

"Yeah. I heard him say something about getting a second chance with you. And going to Las Vegas and something about a wedding. Then your father was all 'oh, I'm so happy to have you in the family' and 'the four of us will have so much fun in Las Vegas.'"

Shannon didn't know whether to laugh or scream. "You thought I was going to Vegas with Jeremy? Why would I do that? I told you it was all in the past with him."

"I know, but your father seemed so happy about it and sounded like he was planning things with you. I thought … "

"You thought I was going to Vegas with Jeremy to make my father happy? Really?"

"I know. I was an idiot. But I kept remembering how much you said you wanted to have a real father in your life and how you kept trying to make him see what a good daughter you were so he'd be the kind of father you wanted. And I thought … "

"I'm not sure 'thought' was any part of this, Leo. More like really bad overreaction." Shannon wanted to be angry. Had a right to be angry. But after what she'd thought about him … wasn't she just as guilty of overreacting? "Why didn't you say something when you called?"

"I did. I said you must be really busy with your plans for the wedding and Las Vegas and the Fourth and everything."

"And *that* was supposed to let me know what you thought you heard?"

"I guess not. It wasn't until Powell told me … "

"*Powell* told you? Damn it to hell, I asked her not to call you." This she knew how to process. Powell was always getting herself into everyone else's business, and it pissed Shannon off.

"Don't be mad. She kept her promise not to call me. She tracked me down to Firehouse when I was there the next day. And she reamed me a new one."

Shannon couldn't hide her smile. "I'd like to have heard her. From a safe distance, of course."

"She almost backed me into the glory hole, wagging her finger at me and yelling. I thought my mom was the expert at lecturing but Powell is much better. Anyway, Powell told me what I didn't hear because I left after I heard your dad and your ex. About how you threatened Jeremy with a restraining order and told your dad off."

"I wonder why she didn't come running back to report to me? It's not like her to keep quiet when she has such juicy information."

"I asked her not to say anything. I wanted to tell you—and apologize. But when I came to pick up the glass and do a *mea culpa*, you were so mad you all but threw me off the porch. Not that I blame you. I was pretty cold on the phone."

"I'm still defrosting my ear." Shannon took his hand and laced her fingers through his, so happy at what she was hearing she had to suppress a giggle. "Why didn't you try again?"

"I wanted to do it in person, so I could see your face, see if you really believed me. I hung around yesterday after I finished work hoping to see you but … " Leo shrugged his shoulders as if he expected she knew why he hadn't tried then.

"But your ex showed up and I saw her with you. I thought she was picking up where you two left off since you're going to be famous and all. That's probably why I'm not as mad about what you thought as I might have been. I did the same stupid thing."

He brushed a piece of hair back from her face. "Cathy was honestly there for the work, not me. She's with someone else now.

I saw you walking home from work and figured you saw the two of us together. It seemed like it would be a lost cause trying to talk to you."

"What changed your mind?"

"The way you reacted this morning. I knew it wasn't only because the glass was broken. It had to be you still felt something for me." He took her chin in his hand. "So, I have a question to ask … "

Shaking off his hand, she said, "Wait. Before we get there, it's my turn."

"Your turn?"

"Yeah." She took a deep breath. "I did see you with Cathy. And I did wonder about it. But I also thought you'd been using me to get your permits."

"I know. Powell accused me of it."

"Crap. She spills the beans on me but protects what she knew about you. Some best friend she is."

"Don't be mad. If she hadn't come after me … well, I don't know if I'd be sitting here now," Leo said.

"Sitting here with a question to ask me, I believe. That's what you said before I interrupted you."

"Yes, I do have something to ask. Was I right?"

"About what?"

"Do you still have feelings for me?"

"Oh, Leo, of course I do. I love you." She put her hand over her mouth when it was too late to keep the words from spilling out.

If a grin could spread from a forehead to a chin, Leo's did. "Thank God. I thought it was only me in love."

"Really? You love me?"

"Yeah. I love you." He tugged at her hand, still interlaced with his. "Come here. You're way too far away."

She went eagerly, her mouth wanting his, her whole body waiting for his touch.

It started out as a soft, gentle kiss but what they immediately generated between them turned it hot, demanding. His tongue explored her mouth fully, thoroughly, and repeatedly as if to make sure nothing had changed since the last time they'd kissed. When he seemed sure it was all as he'd left it, he nibbled at her lip then kissed it to take away any hurt he'd caused. His arms were around her as he leaned back against the arm of the porch swing, bringing her with him, the length of her body now against his. It was like coming home, where she belonged. She wanted to get caught up in the moment, caught up in him.

But she couldn't. They had to stop. Her hands on his chest, she pushed back at him. "We can't do this. Not here. Not tonight."

His frustrated sigh said he knew exactly what she meant. "We can't even have make-up sex, can we? Not now." With another sigh he sat up. "Perfect ending to the rest of the week, huh?"

Kissing him lightly on the forehead she said, "But we can go get the coffee and then sit here and hold each other for a few hours. Maybe the bad guy will show up early."

Chapter Twenty

Two hours later, Shannon was asleep and so was the arm Leo had cradled around her. She looked so sweet lying against his arm he didn't want to disturb her. There had been nothing to see across the street on the parade grounds, so he'd spent his time looking at her through sleepy eyes and enjoying the view.

After they'd gotten the talking and a bit of kissing out of the way, they'd gone inside for coffee and the flashlights he'd asked for. In her pantry, she'd proudly showed off the most complete emergency kit he'd ever seen, which happened to include three huge flashlights. He teased her all the way from her pantry back to the front porch, threatening to move in with her at the first sign of an impending disaster.

They'd settled on the porch swing and split a pot of coffee. But it hadn't been enough. She'd drifted off to sleep, and he'd had a hard time keeping his eyes open. He figured it must be after midnight. Maybe he could close his eyes for a minute or two.

He didn't know how long he dozed, but something woke him with a start. A loud noise. A dim light. Gently he shook Shannon.

"Baby, wake up," he whispered. He had his hand close to her mouth to quiet her if she made a noise, but she sat up yawning.

"What's going on?" she asked.

"There's something—someone—across the street."

Another sharp sound echoed across the parade grounds. "That's the same noise I heard last night. Like a backfire," Shannon said.

"Do you have your phone?"

She held it up. "Right here."

"I'll see what's happening. You stay on this side of the fence. Call 911 and tell them there's an intruder."

"You're not going over there alone. I'm going with you."

"I need you to be safe," he said.

"And I need to be with you to make sure you don't get in trouble."

"Shannon, please. I'm not going to get in trouble. Whoever is over there is more intent on destroying the glass than on dealing with me. I'll be fine."

"He's got a gun." She hugged him. "You could get hurt."

"I won't get hurt. Come on, we're wasting time."

A third shot sounded.

"If we don't stop him, he'll destroy everything we did this afternoon." Without waiting for her to agree, he bounded down the steps, flashlight in hand, and ran across the street.

• • •

Shannon watched Leo disappear into the darkness. Afraid for his safety, her hand was shaking hard enough when she tried to call 911 that she could barely punch the numbers. The operator told her to stay where she was; the police were on the way without lights or sirens.

But when she heard another shot, she disobeyed both the operator and Leo and ran as hard and fast as she could to the parade grounds.

• • •

Staying in the shadow of the trees near the visitor center, Leo walked carefully through the inky darkness, hoping he didn't step on anything noisy and alert whoever was shooting at his glass. His eyes already accustomed to the lack of light, he could see the shape of a person not too far ahead. Then he heard someone muttering. He stopped to hear what the man was saying—and it was a man, he was sure now—but it was unintelligible.

He moved again, following the sound of the muttering, knowing the next part would be the trickiest. He had to break from the cover of the trees and confront a man with a gun. Maybe Shannon was right. Maybe he should wait for the police to arrive.

Then he heard a sound he recognized—the lever on a bolt-action rifle being pulled. The guy was about to shoot again.

Leo charged from the shadows and hit the shooter in the midsection. The sound of a rifle going off close to his ear stunned him.

• • •

Shannon saw the dark shapes of two cars approaching from either end of Officers' Row—the police, thank God. Then from near the tree line to the east, she heard first a man grunt loudly, then a gunshot.

The police could find their way by themselves. Leo was in trouble.

• • •

When he was a kid, Leo had been in plenty of wrestling contests with his older brothers. Those matches had been nothing like this. The man with the rifle seemed to be shorter than he was but the guy was fit and fighting dirty. Knees, hands, elbows, fingers, fists—everything he could throw at Leo, he did. However, Leo had three things on his side: his size advantage, his determination to protect his work, and luck. The guy slipped and fell. Leo pounced. Jumped on top of him, grabbed the guy's wrists, and held them in an unbreakable hold.

"Who the hell are you and why the hell are you wrecking my work?" he demanded when he had the man subdued.

"Who wants to know?" the shooter snarled.

From behind them, Shannon's voice said, "Leo, are you okay? I heard a shot."

"I'm fine but I dropped the flashlight. Who is this asshat?"

When she shone her flashlight onto the face of the vandal, Leo was so startled he almost loosened his hold on the man. Almost. When the surprise passed, he tightened his grip so he didn't give in to the next reaction, which was to punch the living daylights out of him.

Shannon was apparently equally at a loss for words. She could barely get out the man's name. "Jer … Jeremy? What … why …? I don't understand."

His eyes wild, Jeremy Vincent spit in Leo's direction then began to scream at him, "You fucked up the best deal I've ever had. Because of you Shannon won't go to Vegas with me. And if I can't get her to Vegas, I won't get a cut of Marty's inheritance. You deserved to have your work ruined."

"What inheritance?" Shannon asked.

"The half million your grandfather left to Marty if he made an effort to get you back in his life. The proof to the lawyer who's handling the estate was that you take part in his wedding. Marty made a deal with me—fifty thousand if I got you there. But because of this fucker, I'm screwed and so's Marty. The money will go to some charity now."

"You're selling Shannon short, Jeremy. I had nothing to do with her decision. She made up her mind all on her own."

"That's not possible. She'd never do it on her own. She wanted him to pay attention to her too much. You convinced her to do it. So you had to pay."

Before Shannon could say anything, the sound of running footsteps and a man saying, "Don't anybody move," announced the arrival of the police.

Leo could tell from the unsteadiness of the flashlight beam on Jeremy's face that Shannon's hand was shaking. He didn't know if she was scared, angry, or just confused. He knew he was mad as hell that this jerk had not only wrecked his work but had insulted Shannon and confirmed the worst about her father.

"What's going on here?" the first officer to arrive asked. "Who are you?" He moved his flashlight beam over the three people in front of him. His colleague did the same when he got to them.

"Thank you for getting here so quickly," Shannon said. "I'm Shannon Morgan, the one who called 911." She squinted into the light from the cop's flashlight. "You sound like one of the officers I talked to yesterday."

"Yeah, I'm Officer Tomlin, Ms. Morgan. What's going on?" he repeated.

Shannon and Leo gave the Cliffs Notes version of what happened, while the second officer secured Jeremy's .22. After Leo got off him, Jeremy was secured, too—in cuffs. He went with the officer to his patrol car.

Shannon and Leo led the first officer to her house where she made another pot of coffee. The two of them gave a more detailed report of what happened. A half hour later, the cop left.

Leo watched the patrol car pull away from the curb then closed and bolted the door before turning to Shannon who was sitting on the couch. "He's gone. It's all over. Finally."

Shannon said nothing. He thought he could see tears beginning to fall down her cheeks. "Are you okay, baby?"

She still said nothing.

He sat beside her and took her in his arms. As soon as her head was on his shoulder, she broke into sobs. When the tears had subsided, she said between gulps and hiccoughs, "You're right. Everything's over. I have to face the fact I never had a father and never will. Everything I tried to do to get him in my life was a waste of my time. I was stupid and foolish and … "

"Brave enough to make yourself vulnerable and courageous enough to go after what you needed and … "

"You don't have to make me sound like a hero. Heroine. Whatever. I'm more like comic relief."

Leo pushed her away so he could look her in the eye. "Very few people I've ever known would have the guts to do what you did. You went after what you wanted. And when you finally realized you'd never be treated the way you deserved, you cut your losses. Be sad about losing the chance with your dad but don't beat up on yourself. It wasn't your fault it didn't work out. It was his. He doesn't deserve you."

She went into the kitchen and came back with tissues. "He was just using me to get the money. I'm sure he wouldn't have had anything to do with me after he got it. What do you want to bet he drops Louise now that he won't have a wedding to prove to the lawyer we're reconciled? I'm not sure I feel more sorry for her if she gets dumped or if he actually marries her."

After a few shuddery sighs, she said, "I think I've cried my last tears over him. I hope I have."

"How can I help change your mood?"

"Tell me there wasn't much damage to your glass."

"I'll have to wait 'til morning to find out for sure, but he seemed to have been shooting at only the one piece. If I'm right, I'll take down whatever's left of the piece and call it good. I can't replace it without blowing more glass, which isn't gonna happen between now and the Fourth."

"I'm so sorry you got caught up in my drama."

"Hey, it's all right." Leo took her chin in his hand and kissed her. "You had no way of knowing what Jeremy and your father were up to."

"I should have seen that Jeremy and my father are peas in a pod. Neither one thinks about anyone but himself. And Jeremy had done crazy things before, like leaving his job and me for the Pacific Coast Trail. But I really didn't think he'd go after you."

Leo smiled. "You know, when I think about it, I might have some sympathy for him. I mean, I was going crazy a couple days ago when I thought I'd lost you."

"So you're saying I should be proud I drive men nuts?"

"Something like that." He kissed her again. "It's late and you need sleep. How about I make some of the chamomile tea and take you upstairs and rub your back?"

"What about Walter? You've been gone an awfully long time."

He dropped a kiss on the top of her head. "I'm sure he'd be happy you thought of him, but I took him to my sister's because I didn't know how long I'd be here. I called her a while ago and made sure it was okay for him to stay the night. We could call and wake them up to ask how he is, if you're really concerned."

She laughed. "I guess it can wait 'til morning."

. . .

By the time Leo made the tea and brought it to her bedroom, Shannon had undressed and was burrowed down under the covers.

"You look like you're about out for the night. Drink your tea and I'll rub your shoulders."

She sat up and took the mug from him, watching to see how he'd react when he realized she was naked under the covers.

"Um, Shannon, don't you want to put something on? I mean ..."

"Don't you like me in bed with you naked?"

"You know I do. But you need sleep."

"I need you, Leo." She put the mug on the bedside table and reached out her arms to him. "I've missed you."

Leo was out of his clothes in record time and under the sheet with her, pressing his bare chest against her breasts, skin to skin, heat to heat.

"I missed you, too, Shannon. I never want to be without you again."

She took his face in her hands, knowing the desire in her eyes matched what she saw in his. "Never again. We'll always be together. You. Me." She paused for a heartbeat or two. "Walter."

Leo threw back his head and laughed long and hard, joy mixed with relief and love. "I knew it. I knew it was my dog keeping you interested."

"What're you going to do about it, hot shot?"

"This. I'm going to do this." Sliding his hands down to her hips, he pressed his erection against her body; she ground her hips against him in response. When he lowered his mouth to hers and claimed her with a hot, wet kiss, she moaned her pleasure. It was as if they'd been apart months, not days, the need for him was so sharp, so all-encompassing. She knew he felt the same need, could feel it in his kiss, in his hands roaming her body, caressing, bringing heat to every inch he touched. With his knee, he separated her legs and settled himself between them. "And there's nothing you can do about it."

"Oh, God, I hope not." She pulled him to her with eager arms.

His kisses felt like the sweet, soft brush of butterfly wings at first, but in only a few moments, desire took over where sweetness had been. He locked his mouth on hers, nipping and nibbling at her lips. She returned the kiss, sucking at his lower lip, exploring his mouth with her tongue, tangling, slipping, sliding in a sensuous dance with his.

When he moved from her mouth to her neck, she arched toward him to encourage him to keep going, to salve the ache in her breasts with his mouth. He needed little encouragement. With one hand he massaged her nipple into a hard, pebbly point. With his mouth, he licked and suckled the other.

But even that wasn't enough. She pushed on his shoulders, directing him to the other ache, the one between her legs, where all the heat from his kisses had migrated, where she was almost frantic to feel him touch her, kiss her, love her.

Slowly, carefully, sinuously he began to lick the folds of her sex. Before he had barely touched her clitoris, she came in a spectacular climax. She was still reeling from it when he whispered, "Protection. Shannon, do you have any protection?"

"Umm, protection. Yes. Bedside table."

She never heard the drawer open or the packet ripped. She didn't see him cover himself. All she knew was on the downside of one climax he had thrust inside her body and was finessing her back up the slope to another. It didn't take long. This time he was with her. And the fireworks were amazing.

Chapter Twenty-One

The Fourth of July weather was better than anticipated, sunny with a few clouds but no rain in the offing. Shannon ate breakfast at five then dressed in her usual July Fourth clothes—navy blue walking shorts, red sandals, a white halter-necked top with its own wrap-around tie belt—and walked to work. Which meant crossing Evergreen Boulevard to the parade grounds on what was the longest workday of her year. She joined the work crew at six and knew she'd be lucky to get home by midnight.

Her first job was to make sure the main stage for the live music was ready for the noon start. It was easy to check off her "to do" list—the city crews always did a great job. Next, she checked with each vendor in turn, making sure they were happy with things. Or at least with everything she had control of. She put out a couple fires—one vendor didn't get the electricity she'd asked for. Another swore his special folding chair had been stolen by a neighboring vendor and was on the verge of starting a fistfight. Shannon got power to the one and found the chair under the display table of its owner for the other. A couple vendors had the usual concerns about whether there would be enough people to cover the costs of being there, but with the expected 70,000 people coming from all over the region, Shannon assured them they would do just fine.

She didn't have much chance to see how Leo was doing. His plan was to mount the glass in the entrance kiosks with Giles and his friends from Firehouse Glass, so she assumed that's where he was. The information booth he'd staff for the rest of the day was set up. Under a white canopy, he'd placed two display tables covered in a red-white-and-blue patterned fabric. On them were brochures and flyers about the Community Foundation, which had funded his installation, information about local glass studios and hot shops as well as his other work. Posters on foam core board explained the fireworks display.

It was all on track for the 8 A.M. opening.

Shannon was about to sneak across the street for a second cup of coffee when a pair of strong arms circled her waist and snuggled her against a muscular chest, while the owner of the arms and chest nuzzled her neck.

"Good morning, whoever you are," she said.

"Whoever I am? If I lick you like Walter does, will you recognize me?"

"Oh, Leo. I recognize your voice now." She turned with a grin, a giggle, and a kiss. "I'm going to get coffee. Want some?"

"Love some. Do you have enough for three more?"

"No, but I can make enough. Giles and the guys?"

"Yeah. We were finishing up the kiosk at the east end of the street when I saw you. Giles chased me away because he said I was paying more attention to you than I was to the glass. I promised coffee in return."

They got the coffee organized. Leo gave Shannon a tour of the final pieces of glass to be installed. It was marvelous in the daylight. She could only imagine how fabulous it would be as it got dark and the lights began to play on the pieces.

The day went by in a blur. When she wasn't putting out figurative fires with the vendors and artists, or helping get performers to the right place at the right time, Shannon spent time with Leo. It was fun to see the easy way he talked to the curious visitors who had dozens of questions about his glass. He seemed to love explaining the process, especially to kids, and probably filled the classes of every glass teacher in town. Local television stations taped Leo talking about his work and planned to add footage of the lighting when it went live. All the local papers were there, too, as was, to Leo's delight, the Associated Press stringer. She did a long interview with him and promised to get it out on the wire along with photos.

And there was a steady stream of Leo's friends and family who'd come especially to see the installation. Amanda St. Claire, her husband, daughter, and stepsons were there; so were Giles and his boyfriend and all the guys from Firehouse Glass. Cathy and her new boyfriend dropped by. The entire Wilson clan—siblings, spouses, children, and parents—was there in force. The only one missing was Walter. He was in doggie daycare because no animals were allowed on the grounds. And even if they had been, Leo wouldn't have brought him because the sound of the real fireworks would have frightened him.

About eight-thirty, when the natural light began to fade some, Leo brought out his laptop and the big experiment with lighting the glass began. He brought up the program, hit the right keys, and they waited. At first nothing happened. It didn't seem to be working. But then, the lights around them began to flash on and off in a random order. Gradually, more and more people gathered around the places where the glass was hung to watch the show, oohing and ahhing at the sight. Kids ran from one place to another trying to figure out the sequence of the lights. When they realized there was no pattern, they tried to guess which firework would be lit next.

It worked exactly as Leo had envisioned it. The brilliant colors of the glass seemed as bright as the real fireworks, and the quick flash of light from the spot gave the impression of an explosion. Even the music from the group performing on the main stage seemed to work with his plan.

A few minutes before ten, Leo shut off the display to disappointed sounds from the crowd. But they weren't disappointed for long.

"Look. It's officially the Fourth of July," Shannon said as the sky lit up with various colors and shapes and the sound of the explosions reverberated for blocks. "The real fireworks have started."

Leo pulled her onto his lap and kissed her temple. "No, baby, the real fireworks will be later, at your house."

And they were.

"He knows more than he told me. I can see it on his face. But how the hell can I get him to say it out loud?" Fiona McCarthy muttered to herself, frowning at the notes she'd hastily scribbled after her lunch with a just-departed Senate staffer. Her frustration at her inability to get more out of him was at stratospheric levels. If only she had the nerve to chase him across Capitol Hill and stick to him like a tick until he told her what she wanted to know.

She was enjoying the image of riding piggyback on the staffer, yelling her questions in his ear while he tried to go about his business, when a male voice interrupted.

"Fiona? I don't know if you remember me. We met about six months ago in Portland." The man belonging to the voice was standing beside her table, a leather jacket in one hand and a battered messenger bag slung over his other shoulder.

When she looked up she quickly shifted to what she hoped was a welcoming expression. "Of course I remember you, Nick. We met at your sister's house, Danny and Jake's engagement party."

She was not likely to forget him. Six-feet-something of broad-shouldered, slim-hipped male. Chestnut brown hair tamed with some sort of product to keep it tousled and in place at the same time. Carefully maintained fashionable stubble, which didn't manage to hide dimples when he smiled, as he was doing now. Sleepy, just-got-out-of-bed hazel eyes capable of melting the knees or any other part of a woman's anatomy.

Add a small gold hoop earring and a gold stud in his left ear, cargo pants he might have had tailor-made, a shirt setting off a better set of chest muscles than any she'd ever seen, (dressed or undressed) and if she hadn't known it before, she knew from seeing him she wasn't in Oregon any more. No one in Portland looked this good.

Ah, yes. Portland. Where her friend Amanda—his sister—lived. The sister who called him *baby* brother. The baby brother who was, from the way Amanda talked, barely out of his teens. Since Fiona didn't think she was old enough to qualify as a cougar, it meant her less than platonic thoughts about Nick made her a cradle robber. Not how she wanted to think of herself. Which was the important point to keep in mind; not how hot he looked.

It was also important to keep in mind how she'd met him. He'd blown into Oregon on an unannounced visit and proceeded to command—no, *demand*—the attention of everyone at a party he hadn't been invited to. Then, just before she left the party he'd done the "we should get together sometime" thing with her. Of course, he never asked how to get in touch with her. Not that she'd have given her number or address to him. Probably.

At the party he kept saying he didn't want to hog the spotlight, but he didn't do much to keep it from happening. Just like every other picture taker she knew, he thought his glamorous overseas assignments made him a star. Probably even a better reporter than the wordsmiths like her who pecked away at their computers all day in a nice safe office. The hell it did. Journalism wasn't about photographs; it was about words, stories that changed people's lives and opinions. If he wanted to move people with images, he should have majored in film studies.

Of course, if he had, his sexy good looks would have probably earned him an Oscar by now and she'd be even more annoyed with him.

Oops. He looked like he'd said something during her mental rant. "Sorry, it's noisy in here. I didn't quite hear you," she said trying to cover for her inattention.

"I said, I'm flattered you remember me," Nick said.

"Reporters never forget interesting people with fascinating jobs who might be a good source for a story someday," she said. *There. That should put him in his place.*

His smile turned into a semi-serious frown. "Ouch. I was hoping I was memorable for something more than my potential as an interview."

Was he really flirting? She couldn't believe it. "Doesn't 'interesting' and 'fascinating' count for something?" Waving at the empty chair across from her, she asked, "Have you had lunch? I'm finished, but if you'd like to join me…"

"I've eaten but I'll never turn down a cup of coffee with a beautiful woman." He draped his jacket on the back of the chair, sat and flagged down a server.

"How did you recognize me out of context?" Fiona asked. "I'm not always good at it." *Maybe if she led by example, he'd keep his ego at bay and his flirting on a low flame.*

After he ordered coffee, he answered her question. "It would be hard to forget you. The expression on your face when my niece asked during the toasts if Jake was going to plant a seed in Danny to make a baby is indelibly etched on my mind."

Something she, too, had to acknowledge wasn't easy to forget. "I thought you were the one who looked surprised."

With a sinfully sensuous smile he said, "No, I'd heard vague rumors about sex before then. Are you sure you weren't startled?"

"Not about sex—I've done a story or two about it in my career. Although I was surprised to find out how much four-year-olds know about the subject these days."

"I have a feeling my brother-in-law was not too happy with my sister for giving their daughter that little piece of information." The server interrupted, placing Nick's coffee in front of him with a flourish. "Are you in D.C. for business or pleasure?" he asked when the man was gone.

"A little of both. I was coming back east on vacation, for a wedding on the Eastern Shore of Maryland this weekend, in St. Michaels, and decided to make some appointments on Capitol Hill tracking down a couple stories. On my own dime, of course. The paper barely pays for mileage to Salem to cover the legislature these days." *Unlike your foreign junkets, five star hotels, and fancy banquets with important people.*

"How long will you be here?"

"Not quite a week, broken up with the weekend in Maryland."

"I just got back in town from an assignment, but when I sort out my schedule maybe we could have dinner before you leave."

"You're sweet, but it's not necessary. You must have a ton of things to catch up on." *And none of them include amusing yourself with me.*

"It would be my pleasure. Not only do I eat dinner on a regular basis, but I prefer good company while I do. Do you have a favorite restaurant in town?"

"Actually, I usually end up eating at my hotel or having room service."

"If you give me your cell phone number, I'll call and we can expand your horizons."

For a half hour, until he had to leave for a meeting, they drank coffee and talked about the people they knew in common and their jobs—his as a photojournalist, hers as an investigative reporter for *Willamette Week*, Portland's alternative newspaper.

It was a good thing they were covering familiar ground because in spite of the fact he irritated her with his extra helping of self-assurance, Fiona couldn't deny how damn attractive he was, which made it hard to concentrate on what he was saying. He was a smart and entertaining conversationalist, all right. But she was more interested at *looking* at his mouth than in listening to what was coming out of it. With a voluptuous lower lip and a perfect Cupid's bow upper lip, it was a mouth she wouldn't mind having kiss her at the spot right behind her ear or the one at the base of her throat. She stifled a moan at the thought.

Oh, God. He licked a drop of coffee off his lower lip with the tip of his tongue. How could something so simple be so sexy? Before she could rid herself of images of him tasting the inside of her mouth, his eyes caught hers with a look she could swear said he knew exactly what she'd been thinking. Which was not good.

And which switched her attention from his mouth to his eyes. With the longest eyelashes she'd ever seen on anyone—male or female—and the gold flecks flashing in the hazel, she could get lost there, too.

Dear God, there better not be a quiz on this conversation. I'll flunk for sure.

Even repeated silent reminders that he was Amanda's much younger brother couldn't whip her errant thoughts into some semblance of adult behavior. Well, the kind of adult behavior two grown-ups demonstrated in public. The other kind, the private kind, was what she wanted to suppress.

She tried mental math. She was thirty-two. He looked like he was in his twenties, which, from Amanda's comments about when he graduated from college, would make him maybe twenty-two or twenty-three. Being this attracted to someone who was practically a teenager felt…well, it felt naughty.

Or exciting.

Whoa, reining in imagination here.

Even if he had spent most of the party at Amanda's home chatting her up, she didn't think the reason was any more complicated than they'd been the only single people there and had related jobs. Even without the age thing, she was sure someone who traveled the world for his job would find a girl from Tacoma, Washington, who'd never been out of the country, fairly uninteresting. And then there was the "I'll call you" thing, which hadn't happened. Was it any more likely to occur this time?

She tuned back into the conversation in time for him to ask for her cell number, again, and to promise to call as soon as he got a couple things on his schedule straightened out.

As she watched him walk toward the door, Fiona reminded herself not to hold her breath waiting for the phone to ring. What was more important was digging the information she was after out of the staffers she would be talking to on the Hill. She went back to reviewing her notes, the sexy, young photographer relegated to the same place she'd put him after the party in Portland—to the back of beyond.

•••

Nick St. Claire left the restaurant near Capitol Hill where he'd been listening to a pitch about a possible piece of work very, very pleased with himself. He'd arrived back in town two days earlier after covering another tribal clash in Indonesia. There wasn't much on his plate until his next assignment in a couple weeks other than the opening of a show of his work at a gallery in Alexandria. Then he got his usual "let's-check-on-baby-brother-Nicky" phone call from Amanda, and she casually mentioned Fiona's presence in D.C.

Amanda couldn't have known—at least he didn't think she knew—how her friend, the beautiful redhead with creamy skin and blue-gray eyes, had been his mental companion off and on during several recent photo shoots. Had he met Fiona any other way than through his sister, he'd have already followed up after the party last fall to scout out the territory. But he'd been reluctant. Getting involved with someone who was friends with his sister might not be such a good idea. Much to his dismay, Amanda still babied him, felt it her duty to comment on his life, and picked apart any of the women he dated who she met or heard about through the family grapevine. In short, she interfered to such an extent, he wasn't interested in having her know he found her friend attractive; wasn't sure how he could ever find a way to test the waters with Fiona to see how warm they were as long as she was in Portland where his sister was.

But Fiona was hard to forget. She was smart, she was funny, and she was great to talk to. Although he had to confess he wasn't exactly looking for interesting conversation at the moment. After a month of living in mud, eating bad food, and avoiding Toyota pickups full of roaming groups of armed rebels, he wanted something more basic: dinner at a nice restaurant with a beautiful woman followed by dessert in his bed. And Fiona might just fill the bill. Today, even in the Ms. Business Professional black suit with the lacy bit under her jacket modestly covering up her cleavage, he could see curves he wouldn't mind exploring further.

When Amanda said Fiona was on his turf, he decided he'd track her down if he had to call every hotel near Capitol Hill and stalk every restaurant hangout for legislative staffers. It turned out he didn't have to search anyplace. He ran into her as if it were meant to be.

He had her phone number. His sister was nowhere in sight. He'd have Fiona all to himself for a week. A week to play around with someone hot and sexy until he got back to his real life—the one occasionally featuring mud and armed rebels. Sometimes the planets aligned just right.

• • •

On her way out the door of the Hyatt on Capitol Hill next morning, Fiona's phone rang. Sure it was either a confirmation of an appointment or a cancellation; she hurriedly dug through her purse and pulled it out. The voice at the other end of the call was a surprise.

"Morning, Fee. It's Nick. It's not too early to call, is it?"

"No, your timing's good. I'm just on my way to the Hill."

"Are you free for dinner tonight?"

"Tonight? Oh, I'm sorry, I can't. I've got a reception to attend."

"Those things never have enough food to qualify as dinner. How about meeting after the reception?"

What the hell was going on? Why was he suddenly so anxious to see her? He hadn't bothered to contact her after they met in Portland. Why was he pushing to spend the evening with her in D.C.? There had to be some reason other than the need to eat dinner.

"This one always does. And you don't have to…"

"I told you—I want to. Please?"

As much as she hated to admit it, even through the phone the husky timbre of his voice sent shivers up her spine. "How about you join me at the reception? It's open to guests. Put on by a group from the Northwest. They invite press people from all over the Northwest every year along with the entire delegation. They put on a good show I hear; lots of regional wine and smoked salmon, among other things. I've always wanted to attend and this year not only am I in town but I have an excuse. Some of my contacts will be there."

"Good smoked salmon? I'm there. Where and what time?"

"It's in 902 in the Hart building. I'll be there about six-thirty."

"Hart building—on the Senate side?"

"Yeah, the ever popular Hart SOB—Senate Office Building."

"Meet you there and then we can have dinner after."

"It might be late getting out."

"It's okay. I've been allowed to stay up past nine for the past year or so. See you tonight."

She closed her phone, threw it in her purse, and walked toward the Hill, her step as snappy as the sound the flags on the Capitol made as they rippled in the spring breeze. It had taken way too long to get past the debacle of her last relationship. Maybe the attention of a sweet young thing might be exactly what she needed for a warm-up before she threw herself into the dating game again. Even if said sweet young thing was a bit arrogant and way too sure of himself.

Now, if only her appointments worked out as well.

Also check out these books by Peggy Bird:

Beginning Again

Loving Again

Together Again

Trusting Again

Believing Again

In the mood for more Crimson Romance?
Check out *Just My Type* by Synithia Williams at
CrimsonRomance.com.

www.ingramcontent.com/pod-product-compliance
Lightning Source LLC
Chambersburg PA
CBHW010311100726
47905CB00011B/3287